# Haints, Haunts, and Hallowed Hills

Edited by Linda Barnette

Cover Illustration by Karen Tillman and Stephanie Williams Dean
Illustration for "The Prospector's Vindication" by
Hannah Cartner Lavasque
Illustration for "Grim Reaping" by S. L. Keller
Additional Illustrations by Stephanie Williams Dean

These stories are works of fiction. Names, characters, places, and incidents are either the products of the authors' imaginations or are used fictitiously. Any resemblance to actual persons, living or dead, business establishments, events, or locales is entirely coincidental.

ISBN-13 9781074985820

# Table of Contents

# The Prospector's Vindication

Julie Terry Cartner

*Rumors of ghost sightings near Catawba, North Carolina, come and go, but nobody can verify their claims. Still the stories are repeated, generation after generation, told around campfires and inside homes on cold winter nights when the wind roars down the chimney and demands entrance at the old doors and windows, shaking the panes and howling into the night. The families are all gone now. Only the stories remain.*

Clouds stormed across the sun, and thunder rumbled nearby. Jagged streaks of lightning hurtled through the air. Dave felt himself sinking, falling through a black, black void, while images of skeletons with long bony fingers and jagged fingernails grasping at his hands, his arms and his shoulders pulled him down, down, down. Streaks of wispy gray hair swirled around his face, and he couldn't see where he was going. The air was dank, damp, musty, and each breath seemed to come from underwater. Panicking, fighting for air, he struggled against the arms that held him. Choking back a scream, he gasped and squirmed, trying to sit up and catch his breath.

"Dave, wake up!" came the deep voice. "I have a story that I need to tell, and you need to hear." Strong, firm hands grasped his shoulders and shook him.

Opening his eyes with a start and a gasp, Dave found himself looking into deep, intense, stormy-gray eyes framed with dark bushy brows in a face that bespoke honesty, integrity and pain, a face haunted by heartbreak, but a face determined to right a wrong. The man began to speak:

"I am Ezekiel Smith, son of Jedediah and Abigail Smith, great-grandfather to Rebecca, and great-great-grandfather to Isabel,

Izzie to you. I don't have much time, so please don't waste it asking how we're having this conversation. Instead, listen…."

Dave nodded mutely.

"Almost two hundred years ago, I moved my small family to Catawba where I planned to apply for ownership of a few acres of land. I went to a section of land that was not owned by anyone, and walked it off, looking for a good place to plant a garden and fence in grasslands for my stock, just a couple of horses, a cow and a few pigs. I didn't want much, just enough to be able to eke out a living for my family. I knew I'd need running water for the stock and for our household, so I headed towards a stream that eventually fed into a lake. Following the stream, I looked for a place to cross where I wouldn't get too wet. Wading across, my plan to stay dry fell apart when I tripped over a rock and fell in, cursing my bad luck as I got up and dripped my way to the shore. Looking down, I saw something shiny. I reached into the water, picked up a rock, and quickly realized it had a vein of gold in it. Excited, but cautious, I went to town and filed a claim for the property — twenty acres surrounding the place where I'd found the gold.

"What I didn't know was I'd been seen, followed and cheated. Another man, Giles Jenkins, who had been hunting nearby, saw me discover the gold, followed me to town, and, as soon as I left, he'd bribed the clerk to file a claim for him, dated a week earlier than mine. Being shrewd, Giles Jenkins and the clerk decided to put his claim aside and only "discover" it after I had done all the preliminary work. Mr. Jenkins promised the clerk a tenth of the profits from the gold mine.

"Upon learning that the land had no previous owner, I began making my plans. I was thrilled to find an island in the lake and determined it would be the perfect place to build a cabin, a safe and cozy home. As much as I wanted to start working the claim, I put my priorities in the right order and built a cabin for my wife, Elizabeth, although I always called her Liz, Lovely Liz. She was expecting our first child, and I wanted to make sure she had a roof over her head before the baby arrived, Izzie's great-grandmother, was born. Putting my excitement on hold, I cleared land on the island and built a cabin then cleared and fenced land for my stock.

Before I knew it, the house was finished. Liz and I moved in, and we began to make our house a home. Soon, she gave me a beautiful gift, our son, Ernest. Life was good. Of course, as soon as I could, I started working the claim, and lo and behold, I found the gold ore! Rushing home to tell my wife, I didn't realize that once again, I'd been watched.

"Giles Jenkins had decided to let me do the hard work and waited until I found the ore to step in and take over. The next day he and several of his friends confronted me; because that's the way bullies are, Dave, they travel in packs. Bullies know they can't beat you one on one, but four against one is never a fair fight. It's kind of like your friend Pete — he won't pick on kids like my great-great-granddaughter, Izzie, by himself — he's always gotten his underlings to do his dirty work for him. He almost had you, Dave, being the new kid in school and all. I'm sure he fed you stories about her and how evil she was, but you realized what you were doing was wrong at the last minute, then you came clean with my girl and got your priorities straight. That's why I chose to tell my story to you. Had you not made the choice you did, this would've been a whole different conversation." For a second, Ezekiel allowed a smile to move its way across his face, a smile that meant anything but happiness, a smile so evil in intent that Dave felt cold chills go down his spine. Once again he breathed a prayer of thanks for making the right decision.

"Anyway, Jenkins came to steal what was mine. Two of his friends, Milton and George, and his brother, Jerome, came with him. Giles calmly informed me that his claim on my property pre-dated mine. He showed me the falsified papers, but truthfully, Dave, I didn't believe or trust him. He was a shifty man and had been known to skirt the edge of the law, and I had a bad feeling, but I didn't know what to do about it. However, I was angry. I had worked too hard to make a home for my lovely Liz and my son and was not going to kowtow to the resident bully and his goons. When I began to argue, Milton and George grabbed me and held me while Jerome started punching me. I managed to break free from Milton and George for a second and lunged towards Giles. He jumped back, slipped, fell backwards, and hit his head on a rock. Just like that he was dead.

"That was all Jerome needed. He and the two other men ran to the sheriff, 'horrified,' to report a murder, telling a tale of my unprovoked attack on Giles. The next morning the sheriff was at my door with a warrant for my arrest. Despite the fact that I was battered and bruised from Jerome's fists, the sheriff would not listen to my side of the story. Giles and Jerome's family had been here for generations, and I was the outsider, the newcomer in town. Why would people believe me when the papers seemed to back Giles' property claim, and Milton and George were willing to testify that I had attacked him in anger when he showed me the papers?

"Faster than you'd believe, I was convicted and put in jail. My beautiful wife came to see me every day, brought me Ernest to hold, and good food to eat, but even with that daily joy, the days stretched endlessly before me. I hated for Liz to see me in that jail cell, and I didn't want my little boy growing up seeing Daddy in prison. I got sick and with no hope of ever being free, I guess I just gave in. Apparently, I went into a deep sleep, and I assume they thought I'd died. They buried me.

"I remember waking up, shivering from the cold and trying anxiously to see — anything — the darkness was beyond description, pure black. And the silence. Not a sound permeated my cage. You see, for a few minutes, I thought I was in my jail cell; more the pity that I was not. I tried to sit up. WHAM! I hit my head. Then I tried to stretch my arms and legs, but when I hit wood almost immediately, my brain strove to figure out what my body already knew. I tried frantically to come up with any other reason, anything but the answer I already knew. Oh, the horror, the absolute horror. It froze my body, my brain, my heart. I was in a casket. Buried alive.

"I have to admit, I lost it. I yelled, I screamed, I cried. I clenched my hands into fists and pounded on the wood that seemed to be closing in upon me. I kicked. I clawed. My fingers became bloody stumps, but I couldn't stop — not until I realized the air was getting thin. I was gasping for breath.

"Suddenly I realized I had been playing with something on my finger. A string! You may not be aware, but folks of old used to tie a string around a dead man's finger before they put him in the casket. The string would run through the casket, through the ground

5

and be attached to a bell above the grave. Sadly, sometimes a person was accidentally buried alive when it appeared as if he were dead. If he awakened in the casket, he could wiggle his finger which would ring the bell. A cemetery worker had the job of listening for the bell. If it rang, he'd quickly get help, and the men would dig up the grave, hopefully saving the person's life. So when I felt the string, I was filled with hope. I furiously wiggled my finger up and down, side to side, every which way. I forced myself to calm down, save the remaining air, and listen intently for the sound of a bell. Nothing. I heard nothing. Waggle. Listen. Nothing. Over and over. Then I heard it. The voice I had grown to hate. Laughter. Then the words, 'Rest in Peace, my friend.' More laughter, fading away. Then silence. The kind of silence that lets you know you are all alone. Nothing and nobody would save me. Jerome had removed the clapper from the bell. The bell moved, so he knew I was trying to ring it, but he'd taken away the ability for it to make sound.

"This was even worse; this was pure evil personified. Jerome ensured that nobody would hear the bell on the off chance that I had been buried alive. Even then, he could have called for help and saved me. But he just walked away. As bad as Giles was, he was motivated by a lust for power and greed. Jerome, on the other hand, was so much worse. He would stop at no lengths to vindicate his brother's death and ensure that he would get the gold, but even more, he derived pleasure from his evil intents. His heart was black.

"Slowly the oxygen went away. I vowed revenge. I got sleepy and had no more will nor reason to fight. I went to sleep and never woke up. I died, knowing my enemy would win everything: my land, my gold, my wife, my child. Despair was the last emotion in my life.

"And that's what happened. Jerome claimed the land as his, found the ore of gold, and pushed my wife further and further into poverty until she had no choice but to marry him or have our child starve to death. She finally gave in to his demands and married him, consigning herself to a life of abuse, treated like a servant rather than a beloved wife. The one thing she refused to do was to change our child's name. Ernest remained Ernest Smith, my wife's one act of rebellion.

"Now years, decades, generations have gone by while I waited for somebody pure of heart to help me. When I saw you and that other boy, Pete, hurt my Izzie, I almost gave up, but then you showed your true colors when you kept him from filming her and returned to help her. You're my last chance. Will you help right an old wrong?"

Dave thought back with shame to how his relationship with Izzie had started:

Hiding in the copse of trees, Dave and Pete held their breaths, waiting for Izzie to come around the bend in the path. They knew it would only be a few minutes, then BAM! She'd step onto the twig and leaf covered hole and go crashing into the mud. Cell phones set and ready to record, each boy had a different mindset.

Stifling his laughter, Pete whispered, "This is gonna be epic. She'll fall, all her books will go flying, and she'll be a muddy mess!" Scowling, he added, "She deserves it. Daddy says her whole family's bad — all the way back to her great-great-granddaddy. He shouldn't 'a tried to steal that property just to get all the gold. It didn't work; we won that fight, but even so, I hate him, and I hate her too — always so stuck up and always making A's. Thinks she's better than everyone else. Serves her right. Just wait till we upload this. It will go viral! I can't wait to see what the other guys say."

Dave forced a grin and agreed, but inwardly he wondered. How was this Izzie's fault? If her great-great-grandfather did steal some property, it certainly didn't have anything to do with Izzie. But he was the new kid in town and was thrilled that Pete and the others were accepting him into their group. Being accepted was so very important in middle school. He hated being an outsider and wanted desperately to fit in. So here he was, about to prank some girl whom he didn't even know and make her life miserable, just because she had the misfortune to have a great-great-grandfather who had, once upon a time, angered Pete's family. Dave's conscience warred with his need to have friends.

Keeping his thoughts to himself, Dave waited beside Pete, allowing his mind to wander. It was just he and his father now; they'd lost Mom to cancer almost a year ago. Dad tried, but his job kept him busy; consequently, Dave was often on his own. They'd had to move, so Dave didn't even have the comfort of his old friends, and making new ones was hard, especially at his age. This left Dave alone often. Sometimes the ache of losing his mother was more than he could bear. Her thick, auburn hair, her warm smile when he would get home from school, and her hugs... but mostly just her — she listened to him, gave him advice, and yes, grinning ruefully, a good kick in the seat when he needed one. His smile fading, Dave couldn't help but think, what would she think of him now? He could hear her, "Treat everyone the way you want to be treated, Dave, and you'll never be ashamed of who you are." How many times had she told him this?

"Hey Dave, wake up!" Pete whispered. "Man, you are chill! We're about to pull the prank of the century, and you're almost asleep," he added admiringly. "Here she comes." Sure enough Izzie came walking around the corner, her chestnut hair shining in the autumn sunlight. Pete and Dave collectively held their breaths, three...two...one...CRASH! Down Izzie went with a scream. Books flying, Izzie hit the ground hard and cried out, then stillness, just like they'd planned, except for one thing. At the last minute, Dave realized just how wrong their behavior was, so he "accidently" tripped and fell into Pete, right when Izzie fell, causing Pete to drop his cell phone; hence, no recording would be hitting the internet.

When Dave looked at Pete and whispered, "Dude, I am so sorry. I tripped over that stick," there wasn't much Pete could do but shrug, and then, as planned, the two boys took off running in opposite directions. As soon as Pete was out of sight, Dave circled around, going back to Izzie, who was still sprawled on the ground crying. "Hey, Izzie," Dave whispered softly, as he gathered up her books and helped her stand up. "Are you okay?" he asked worriedly when he saw her limping.

"I think I sprained my ankle," was Izzie's teary reply. "Thanks for the help, but you'd better run away before my evil contaminates you," she said bitterly. "You're new here, so you might not know about my family, about my great-great-grandfather, Ezekiel Smith, better known as Big Zeke. People say he stole Pete's great-great-grandfather's gold mining rights right after he had found gold on the property. They say the two men had a huge fight, and

Big Zeke killed Mr. Jenkins. Then Great-great-grandpa was sentenced to death, but before he could be hanged, he got sick and died. I think he just gave up. He's buried in the old churchyard near here." She added, "Now you know, so run away like everyone else. They say my blood is tainted with his evil."

"No, let me help you home. Please," he added, when Dave saw the doubt in Izzie's eyes.

"If you're sure...you'll have no chance with our classmates if you're seen with me," warned Izzie.

Hesitating only an instant as he saw his acceptance and social life slip away, Dave took Izzie's elbow and helped her hobble towards her house. At first silence descended between the two as Dave got his thoughts together. Again, hearing his mother's voice in his head, admonishing him, "Deception, Dave, no matter how well intentioned, always festers in your heart," he began talking.

First, he told her of his mother's death, his loneliness and grief, his difficulty moving and starting at a new school, and his desire to fit in, and finally, as he was about to confess his part in the prank, they got to the cemetery where Izzie's great-great-grandfather was buried.

Resting on the stone wall near his grave, Dave took Izzie's hands, looked directly into her eyes and confessed. Concluding, "You know why I went along with it, but that's no excuse. All I can say is, I'm sorry, and it won't happen again." Seeing the tears in her eyes, Dave dropped Izzie's hands and turned to walk away. "I hope you can forgive me one day."

"Dave, wait," Izzie said in a low voice. "What you did was wrong, but I do understand. Sixth grade is hard for everyone, but it's even harder for the new kid. And the rest, your mom...I'm so sorry. I'd like for us to be friends. We can be the two outcasts," she joked in a wavering voice. "But I'll try to understand if you want to pretend like you never talked to me and go hang out with Pete and his friends."

"No, Izzie, I'd like to be your friend," was Dave's simple response. And as soon as he said it, he knew. He really did want to be Izzie's friend, not Pete's. The weight of his earlier actions lifted off his shoulders, and he knew he'd made the right decision.

Smiling with happiness, Izzie showed Dave the grave where Big Zeke and Liz were buried. The grave had the kind of stone with both names on it. "Miss Liz, as everyone called her, never stopped believing in her husband, in his innocence. She swears he didn't steal Mr. Jenkins' claim. Big Zeke was a good man, a good father, a good husband. She firmly stated her faith in him as long as she lived and made sure Ernest knew his real daddy was a good man. She asked Ernest to bury her beside Zeke when her time came and, if he could, to put a husband and wife headstone on the grave. Finally, she asked for a special inscription so people would know she believed in him all the way to the grave. Look," said Izzie, as she pointed to the epitaph still visible on the old marble stone:

*'An honest man here lies at rest*
*As e'er God with his image blest;*
*The friend of man, the friend of truth,*
*The friend of age, and guide of youth.'*

"Robert Burns wrote that. He was a famous Scottish poet," Izzie added. Tears sparkling on her eyelashes, Izzie held her head up proudly. "I'm gonna prove his innocence. I am going to clear my family's name. I never knew him, of course, but I feel connected to him, and I truly believe I'm the one who can do it."

Shaking his head in admiration, all Dave could reply was, "I believe you. How can I help?"

In the days that followed, Dave and Izzie got to know each other better as they explored the old church and cemetery, Big Zeke and Miss Liz's cabin on the island, and the surrounding woods. Dave was especially intrigued by the way they would get to the cabin. It was on an island in the lake, so they stood on a hand-powered ferry and pulled themselves across to the island. He found the pulley system very fascinating and fun. Izzie introduced Dave to her mother. She warned Dave not to mention their quest to clear Big Zeke's name. "She believes in letting go of things and just doesn't understand why I would want to stir up old news. She doesn't realize how mean the kids at school still are."

Izzie and Dave had agreed to meet at the churchyard one afternoon after Izzie finished helping her mother with her chores. Dave had arrived early, and, feeling sleepy, he had stretched out on the grass right beside Izzie's great-great-grandfather's grave where the sun was shining invitingly. Almost immediately falling asleep, he had drifted pleasantly into dreams until he was abruptly jerked awake. Clouds stormed across the sun and thunder rumbled nearby. Jagged streaks of lightning hurtled through the air, and Izzie's great-great-grandfather was shaking him. Returning to the present, Dave looked into Zeke's eyes once again and saw only honesty and pain.

Dave simply said, "What can I do?"

The ghost told Dave where he had hidden the original deed, wrapped in oilcloth and concealed behind a loose rock in the fireplace of the old homestead out on the island, which thankfully still belonged to the Smith family. Jerome's family had claimed the gold mine but had had no interest in the island or cabin. Luckily, Liz had refused to let anything happen to that cabin. She wouldn't live there with Jerome, but she kept it intact so that one day Ernest could live there if he wished. "You'll also find my will, leaving everything to Elizabeth, then Ernest, then Ernest's descendants," he added.

Dave reminded the ghost the document could prove ownership but would not negate the rest of the story including the alleged murder.

Ezekiel agreed, saying "hold on," as he continued the story: "Milton was always as shifty as Pete's great-grandfather, but I always thought George was a more decent guy — a follower, you know. Remember, Dave, if you want to be a follower, that's fine — the world needs leaders and followers, but choose carefully whom you follow.

"Anyway, one Friday, after I had been locked up for several weeks, George came to see me in my prison cell after Liz left from her daily visit. He apologized for his part in what happened and told me he was going to the sheriff to confess. However, George had trouble talking; he stuttered badly, so he was going to write the facts down and give the written confession to the sheriff. He promised he was going home right then to do just that.

"Saying he was sorry again, George promised he'd make it right. That weekend, my spirits were lighter than they'd been since the whole mess started. When Liz came to see me Monday, I told her. Instead of seeing the joy I was expecting, she sobbed, 'Oh Zeke, George was killed Saturday evening — he drowned — he fell through the ice on Miller's pond.'

"It wouldn't surprise me if, rather than accidentally falling, George was pushed. I'm sure Jerome saw him as the weak link and would have killed him rather than risking being caught through George's confession. That's when I gave up, Dave. I knew it was over. Jerome had won. Since then, in the hundreds of years I've had to think, I've always wondered if George wrote down his confession. Since I've been in my ghostly state, I've explored George's house, and I think I found where he might have hidden the confession. I can't get to it. I can pass through solid objects; I can't move them, but you could. If I'm right, the confession is in the root cellar which you can still see behind the ruins of George's house. I think George's spirit lives there; however, our spirits are not allowed to communicate. I don't know why — who would have thought ghosts had so many rules to follow! But you are alive; there are no rules for you.

"So Dave, my boy, it's up to you. Will you help my Izzie and her mom? I know how badly Izzie wanted to clear my name, but I didn't want her to go wandering around by herself. However, the two of you together with spirits so pure... the two of you together, I believe can do anything. All you need to do is find the documents and turn them in to the authorities. The sheriff and his deputies are all new, not connected in any way to the dishonest men of my lifetime. Tell them the story the best you can without mentioning our visit, or they might lock you up," he chuckled. "How about it Dave, will you help Izzie right a two hundred year wrong?"

Dave didn't hesitate. "Yes, Sir, it would be my honor. If the only way to fit in with the other boys is to let a lie stand, then I don't want anything to do with them."

*****

Dave awoke with a start. The first thing he noticed was that it was once again a beautiful, sunny day. Realizing he was lying on the ground beside Ezekiel's grave, he rubbed his eyes, then looked up to see Izzie laughing at him. "Wake up, Sleepyhead!" she giggled.

Dave began, "Izzie, you're not gonna believe this, but…" and he proceeded to tell her the whole story. He concluded, "That's why people say those two places are haunted. They actually are."

"By my great-great-grandfather, how cool is that!" Izzie exclaimed.

The two agreed to keep the story to themselves until they could find the missing papers. They planned to meet the next night after they were supposed to be in bed and go to George's house.

The next night, after telling his father good-night, Dave quietly clambered out of his window, shimmied down the tree outside his room and went to meet Izzie. Armed with flashlights, they crept to the ruins that were once George's house. Agreeing not to talk or shine their lights, the two friends moved stealthily behind the house and found the rocks that used to be the entrance to the root cellar. It didn't take long to find the entranceway, but it did take some time to clear a space for the door to open. At long last, tired and breathing heavily, they finally got to the door, and, with creaks and groans, it slowly gave way under their insistence and crept open. Suddenly, a boom, a flash of light, and a ghostly scream…the two froze for an instant, then took off running. A few seconds later, hiding behind a tree, they gasped for air.

"Did. You. Hear. That?" Izzie gasped.

"Probably the whole town heard it," was Dave's response as he tried to catch his breath. "Let's go home." Grabbing Izzie's hand, he started pulling her towards town.

"No," said Izzie, as she pulled her hand away. "I won't get this close and give up."

"Let's wait till morning then," pleaded Dave.

"You know we can't. People will see us," Izzie stubbornly refused. "We finish this tonight." With that she turned on her heel and headed back to the root cellar.

"Izzie," Dave pleaded, but then ran to catch up with her. "I won't let you do this alone. I'll go with you. But man, oh man…" he started.

"I know! I'm scared too," Izzie exclaimed. "That was something!"

Taking a few minutes to recover, Dave and Izzie talked quietly. When Dave calmed down, he realized what he should have realized immediately. The ghost was George, of course. And George was only trying to keep his promise to Big Zeke by protecting the letter. To be totally honest, Dave was still scared, but it did help a bit to have a name and reason for the ghost. Telling his suspicions to Izzie, Dave then said, "Okay, I'm ready. Are you?"

Receiving an affirmative nod, Dave and Izzie proceeded cautiously to the root cellar. With the door now open, Izzie and Dave gingerly started down the steps. One step, two steps, three steps, then the groaning started. It got louder and louder until it was no longer a groan, it was a scream, and then a shriek, and then they heard the footsteps – coming closer and closer to them. More screaming, more groaning, then an unearthly shriek rent the air as Dave and Izzie took one look at each other, then flew back up the stairs and across the yard.

"It's got to be George; it just has to be," said Izzie, repeating it over and over like a mantra, "but it's still terrifying."

Dave agreed, wholeheartedly, but then, after some thought, he added, "But I find it interesting that he won't, or can't, follow us out here. I know we didn't want to shine our flashlights because we didn't want anyone to see us, but I think we need to turn them on to try to see if he's doing the screaming and moaning. That is, if you want to try again. Because if you don't, Izzie, that is fine with me!"

"We have to. We just have to. I keep getting the feeling this is our last chance, and if we don't find the letter tonight, we never will. Come on Dave, let's do it," begged Izzie. As they started forward one more time, Izzie stopped. "Dave, we have to talk to him. Maybe if you explain who we are and what we're doing, he won't try to stop us."

"You're right, Izzie; we have to try something else, and that might be exactly what we need to do," agreed Dave. When he learns that you are Big Zeke's great-great-granddaughter, he might be nicer."

Approaching the door once again, this time with flashlights breaking up the darkness, they immediately heard a groan, then footsteps. With that, Dave started talking. He explained who they were and what they were doing. He promised they were looking for the letter because Zeke had asked them to do so. Izzie assured the ghost she was Zeke's descendent. As they talked, they kept moving forward until they had traveled down all the steps. With bated breaths they listened for the ghost, but heard nothing, so they quickly started searching the stone wall, looking and feeling for any loose rocks. Finally, Izzie realized they were probably looking too low. Since George had been a tall man, he probably would have hidden the papers higher. Izzie turned to the doorway and started checking the stones that framed the archway. Sure enough, about three-fourths of the way up, she found a loose stone. "Dave, I think I've found it, but I can't get a good enough grip. Please help."

Dave went to Izzie. After several minutes of wiggling, twisting and turning, together the two were able to pull out the loosened stone; then Izzie tentatively reached inside as the two chanted, "Be there, be there, be there!" Reaching as far back as she could, Izzie felt something. Wrapping her fingers around it, she pulled out a packet wrapped in oilcloth. Sure enough, when they opened it under the beam of the flashlights, they could see that the paper was really old, and it started with the words, "If you find this, take it immediately to the sheriff. An innocent man is going to die if the sheriff does not receive this information…"

"This is it," Izzie breathed. "We need to take it somewhere safe, and we need to get home before we get caught for being out all night."

Agreeing, Dave caught Izzie's hand, and they turned to leave — only to stare into the barrel of a gun being held by Pete. "Not so fast. I'll take that," Pete said in a low, tense voice. "I've been following you two all night. I lost you for a while. I thought you were in the ruins of the old house, but then as I was searching inside the old place, I heard you talking, and all I had to do was follow your voices. Thanks for doing all the work for me. Now I can destroy that confession, and nobody will be the wiser. Nobody's going to take the land from my family."

Izzie and Dave froze. What in the world was Pete thinking? A gun? Was it loaded? Would he really shoot them? Could he shoot? What could they do? In tacit agreement, they both quickly turned off their flashlights and sank down to the floor, figuring Pete would have a difficult time shooting them if he couldn't see them. They'd forgotten about the ghost though, and as soon as the room was covered in darkness, the spirit started shrieking once more, this time much to their joy.

Pete screamed, dropped the gun, and tore up the stairs. "What is that?" he screeched, but he didn't wait for their response; he just kept running.

With a mixture of laughter and tears, Dave and Izzie picked up the gun with an old rag, and, with the note, headed to their respective houses. They decided it was time to get some adult help. Waking Izzie's mother and Dave's father, the four met at Izzie's house, and the two friends told their parents the whole story. The four made the decision to go to the island in the morning to collect the final evidence, then take all of it to the sheriff's office and tell the sheriff the edited version — no ghosts. They figured nobody would believe them anyway.

In the morning Dave and Izzie, along with their parents stepped carefully onto the hand-pulled ferry, slid across the gently waving water, and stepped onto the shore of the island. Immediately going to Big Zeke's old cabin, they began their search, and, with the ghost's information, easily found the papers Ezekiel had hidden so many years ago. There were no shrieks this time. Dave and Izzie figured Ezekiel was glad for them to find the papers, since he told them where to look, but George, not knowing them, had been protecting his information from random strangers. Quickly looking at the papers to ensure they were what was needed, the four returned to Izzie's house. Then, to guarantee that everyone had the same information, Izzie scanned the papers onto her computer, and, printing a copy for herself and another for Dave, they then took the original papers, as well as Pete's gun, to the sheriff's office.

When they arrived, Dave and Izzie told the entire story to Sheriff Jonas Martin, only omitting the ghostly visits, then gave him the documents. Amazed, he listened carefully, then examined the papers. He told them that modern technology could date the papers for authenticity and verify the truth. Looking carefully at their faces, the chief saw no hesitation; rather he saw the intrigued faces of two eleven-year-olds who wanted to know exactly how science could do that. Pleased by their reactions, he told Izzie and Dave he'd try to get more information on how it was done, and maybe he could take them with him when he delivered the original papers to the lab.

True to his word, Chief Martin did, in fact, allow Dave and Izzie, with their parents to go to the lab where a scientist was pleased to answer their questions. He promised results within two weeks. About ten days later the news was announced. It would take time to straighten out all the legal and financial issues, but the documents that Izzie and Dave turned in were valid, the property did, in fact, belong to the Smith family, and Izzie's great-great-grandfather was cleared from all blame, innocent of all charges. George's letter told exactly what had happened that day, and it was just as Big Zeke had told Dave. Finally, after over two hundred years, the Smith family's name was clear.

Not long after the announcements were made, Pete's family moved away without a word. Pete had received mandatory institutionalization in a juvenile facility until he turned eighteen, at which point he would be assessed for whether he was still a danger to society. Pete's band of followers fell apart without a leader, and the reign of terror at Izzie and Dave's school ended. An anti-bullying campaign was started, led by Izzie and Dave. Its slogan, "Treat everyone as you would like to be treated, and you'll never be ashamed of who you are," was a tribute to Dave's mother.

One sunny fall day, Izzie and Dave went back to Ezekiel's grave and told him everything that had happened. They didn't see Big Zeke, but the two sat at the gravesite and talked to the stone. Only when Dave was leaving did he feel a warm pat on his back. Did he hear the words, "Well done, my boy," or was that just his imagination? Dave didn't know for sure, but he'd like to think Ezekiel and his mother would be proud of him.

*It is said, in the rolling foothills of Catawba, North Carolina, if you stand quietly along the shore of Lake Lookout, you might catch a glimpse of Big Zeke, working on his gold claim stolen from him almost two hundred years ago. If you're lucky and pure of heart, you might see the Lovely Liz, holding their baby, Ernest, in her arms as she carries a picnic basket to join Zeke for lunch. If you're fortunate enough to see this, you'd see a loving couple embrace, then share a blanket and a lunch. However, if you do not have pure intentions, you will probably see Big Zeke and George, standing shoulder to shoulder, and before you know it, you'll be running for your life as they chase you out of their lovely little town.*

As a child, Julie fell in love with the written word, which led to a lifelong love of reading and writing. At a young age she learned to write down her feelings through poetry, letters, essays, and short stories, when she was too shy to verbalize them. This affinity for the written word led her to an English major. After thirty-eight years of sharing her passion for great literature with high school students, Julie retired. When she's not writing, she spends her time dancing, swimming, and hiking. Julie is currently working on several fantasy fiction stories for young readers.

The Prospector's Vindication

## The Cliff

Gaye Hoots

S arah awoke with a low moan, sensing she was not alone in the room. She could see a vision of her son, Jacob, precariously balanced on the edge of a cliff. He had his back to her and was peering over the cliff, clutching a muscadine vine to steady himself. As Sarah stared in horror, a transparent figure composed of white vapor ran toward Jacob with arms outstretched to push him over the cliff. Sarah's moans were an attempt to alert Jacob to the danger.

She pinched her left forearm several times to be sure she was awake. Sarah followed the same ritual of climbing a few rungs of the ladder to the sleeping loft to reassure herself that Jacob was safe. Her left arm had been covered with bruises for the last month as the visions became more frequent.

Mother and son had moved to the small, one-room, log cabin which had a front door, two small shuttered windows, and a large fireplace two months ago after the death of Jacob's father. Jacob slept in the sleeping loft on a mattress of dried corn shucks, and Sarah slept in a rope bed to the right side of the fireplace. The only other furnishings consisted of a stretcher table and two wooden chairs with hide bottoms. They had brought all they owned in one wagonload.

Their cabin was on a small farm owned by Sarah's in-laws, Isaac and Elizabeth, who lived a mile away in a cabin only slightly larger than hers. When her husband had died of consumption his parents had asked Sarah and Jacob, their only grandson, to move back to the farm where they had raised his father. When Jacob asked his mother to make the move to his grandparents, Isaac had begun restoring the cabin which had remained empty since before he purchased the farm.

Isaac told Sarah the history of the cabin before starting work on it. Isaac had seen a girl a few times at Lutheran meetings who had a child out-of-wedlock. The girl's parents lived in the cabin Isaac and his wife now lived in. When their daughter gave birth to a boy, they moved her from their home to the small cabin to raise the boy alone. The child had been born with a handicap of some nature. His mother kept him in the cabin and did not send him to school, fearing the other children would make fun of him. When he became older, there were rumors that he was dangerous. On one occasion, the boy had run from his home waving his arms and shouting gibberish to two children approaching a footbridge just as the swollen stream washed it away. The children were so frightened they had nightmares for weeks.

Another story was that he had approached children playing near the edge of a field. He ran toward the children again waving his arms and shouting incoherently. This time a bobcat appeared near him and chased the children a few yards until one of their fathers shot it. Shortly after this the mother was found dead of natural causes in the cabin. The son was never seen again. Two or three years later a skeleton was found deep in the woods that surrounded the cabin and was presumed to be his.

The cabin sat empty since the deaths. Isaac bought the farm from the parents of the girl before he was married. Few people mentioned the previous occupants after their deaths. Isaac had felt obligated to tell Sarah the history because she was grieving and under a lot of emotional stress. He did not wish to contribute any cause for concern.

Sarah was pleased to have a cabin of her own. She was not upset by living where a death had previously occurred. Her own parents had died while she was living with them. It was comforting to her and her brother that they died in their own home.

The first four weeks had been busy but pleasant ones. Sarah and Jacob carried water from a nearby spring to the house. They scrubbed the walls, fireplace, and floor. Mother and son brought some canned vegetables and dried herbs with them and stored them on shelves along one wall. Jacob's grandparents had a cow and chickens that supplied them with milk, butter, and eggs. The grandparents also shared the contents of their garden. Jacob picked berries and brought muscadines from the woods behind the cabin.

Isaac gave Jacob a small male puppy, a border collie mix. The twelve-year-old was elated with his present, and he named the dog Shep. Jacob and Shep became inseparable.

Sarah and Jacob had a life filled with hard work as they helped Isaac on the farm, tended gardens, cared for the horses, pigs, cow, and chickens. They had not stopped grieving their loss but became confident they could live independently and rely on each other. Jacob wanted to be able to fill his father's shoes and keep his mother safe. They had a flintlock rifle that was his fathers, and both knew how to use the gun. Sarah had just begun to adjust to her new life when the visions began.

They were always the same. Sarah would awake moaning as she tried to alert Jacob of the presence of the figure composed of vapor. She saw a boy about Jacob's size who moved toward Jacob with an uneven gait. He flapped his hands in front of him and was mumbling something Sarah could not understand. He was always moving away from her, so she saw only the back of his head. Remnants of pants and a loose shirt swirled about him. The apparition always disappeared just before Jacob was pushed over the cliff. Sarah experienced visions two or three nights a week and it began to take a toll on her.

She did not tell Isaac about the visions but did question him about the family who had previously occupied the house. Sarah asked if the incidents involving the boy had been before his death or if he had been described as a ghost. Isaac was concerned but did ask neighbors who had lived in the area before he moved there. He learned that one of the sightings had been a vapor apparition. The story had been told by a young boy, so adults had believed it was the result of an overactive imagination.

Isaac believed Sarah was mourning the loss of her husband and associated the death of the boy who lived in the cabin with her own loss. He didn't press for details but did invite them to stay at his house for a while. He had been taking Jacob with him when he went hunting and fishing. The boy did well fishing, and his use of a rifle was good for a twelve-year-old boy. Isaac had taught Jacob to milk the cow, and he was a big help around the farm. Sarah encouraged Jacob to help his grandfather and felt Jacob was safe while with Isaac. She wanted to maintain their independence but thanked Isaac for his invitation.

Sarah continued to experience the visions but spent less time consciously thinking of the threat as Jacob became better acquainted with the area and more confident in his own skills. They lived in Lincoln County, North Carolina, a place where wild game was abundant, and the South Fork Catawba River was a two-mile walk. Jacob brought fish home every week. His pup followed everywhere he went. Sarah had quizzed Jacob and Isaac about cliffs or high overhangs in the area. but they had not reported any.

Life was good except for the apparitions disturbing Sarah's sleep. She wanted to warn Jacob but not frighten him. Sarah did tell him she had a scary dream about him falling over a cliff but did not mention the apparition. "Promise me you will not get near a cliff," she implored Jacob. Jacob had no problem promising as he had not seen any cliffs or steep overhangs in the area he and Isaac hunted and fished. He did not explore new areas when Isaac was not with him. Jacob felt safe and hoped his mother would trust his judgment.

Sarah began to wonder if the ghost were drawn to Jacob because they were about the same age, and both boys lived with their mothers in the cabin. Isaac told her the neighbors had feared the boy because he was different. They had warned their children to stay away from him, and his own mother tried to keep him with her to avoid problems with the neighbors. No one knew if he really posed any danger or simply became excited when he saw other children. The whole story was disturbing to Sarah. The thought of a young girl, barely a woman, attempting to raise a child with physical and perhaps emotional limitations alone and isolated from her community was heart breaking. There had been a lot of speculation about the child's father, but no one had a clue who the father was.

Each night Sarah prayed for Jacob's safety and for the mother and child who had lived in their cabin, praying that their souls would be at peace. She also prayed for Jacob's father's soul and for God to help them adjust to life without the man she loved so dearly and for the safety of her in-laws and neighbors. When the visions appeared, Sarah repeated the prayers and tried to sleep.

Sarah did not allow herself the luxury of tears at night because she did not want Jacob to hear her cry. She had begun to release some of her grief during the day when Jacob was with Isaac or fishing. Sarah would sit in a chair by the fireplace and remember how happy they had been before her husband became ill. She could pretend for the moment that her husband was out fishing with Jacob and would be returning soon. Then reality would grip her, and she would sit sobbing until she could regain her composure. Sarah had begun to sense a presence while she was grieving. Could it be that of her husband? Sometimes she would catch a glimpse of a shadow over her right shoulder. This was almost a comforting presence. The episodes of the apparition pushing Jacob over the cliff decreased but did not leave entirely.

Jacob was also grieving the loss of his father. He wanted desperately to be able to fill his father's shoes and protect his mother. His grandparents were a great comfort. His grandfather had continued to help him improve his hunting and fishing skills. They often ate supper together at the end of the day. His grandmother was a good cook and gave him food to take home to his mother. Jacob knew his mother was hurting but trying to keep up a brave front for him. He tried to keep her from worrying.

Jacob loved his puppy and took him on all his forays into the forest. He would often gather the pup into his lap to play with him. One afternoon as the pup was licking his face, Jacob sensed someone or something watching him. It was disquieting, but he did not feel threatened. Perhaps it was a deer or some other animal he reasoned. This began to happen more frequently and always when he was frolicking with Shep. Jacob did not mention this to his mother or to Isaac. He did not want to worry Sarah and would feel foolish telling Isaac, so he didn't.

One morning, Jacob ate a breakfast of eggs and corn fritters his mom cooked for him. She wrapped some corn fritters and fried side meat for his lunch. Jacob was going fishing and would spend the whole day in the forest. He put his lunch into his knapsack, picked up his reed fishing pole, and hugged his mother goodbye. Sarah waved goodbye until they disappeared into the woods. Jacob planned to return with fish for supper. Fresh fish always pleased his mom. He knew the many chores would keep her busy while he was gone.

He whistled happily with the dog at his heels. They headed to Jacob's favorite fishing spot where the fishing was usually good. Jacob put the fish he caught on a string and left them in the stream to keep them alive. When he stopped to eat lunch, he shared with Shep and again had the feeling someone was watching. The fish did not bite as well in the afternoon, and Jacob dozed. When he awakened, the pup was in a frenzy barking at something in the brush. Shep dashed off after his prey.

Jacob saw dark, threatening clouds had gathered. He retrieved his string of fish, picked up his fishing reed and knapsack, and called to the dog. He could hear him barking but Shep did not come when called. Jacob began shouting and followed the pup's bark. Shep was traveling upstream giving full voice. The boy had no choice but to follow his dog. The storm clouds were now as dark as night as Jacob tramped through the brush. He could not keep up with Shep.

Suddenly, Shep yelped and then began to cry like the pup he was. Jacob pushed on toward the sound of his cries. It took a while to close the distance between them. When he was closer to the sound of the cries, Jacob pushed through the muscadine vines and brush as the roar of the river became louder. He was getting closer to the cries as the ground under his feet became spongy. Jacob dropped his fish, knapsack, and reed, as he grabbed a large muscadine vine to steady himself. He pushed the vines apart and saw the river and a waterfall. Looking down, Jacob saw he was on a cliff about twenty feet high a short distance above the waterfall. It was dark, and he could see Shep about halfway down the bank below him. The dog had landed on the roots of a tree and was clinging precariously to the bank. "I'll get you out boy," Jacob shouted as he felt a hand on his shoulder. His head began to swirl as everything went black.

*****

Sarah had worked in the cabin and yard into the late afternoon. She sponged herself off and sat down in front of the fireplace with a cup of tea. It was comforting. Sarah lapsed into daydreams of what might have been if her husband had lived.

Suddenly she was wide awake. She saw Jacob on the now familiar cliff, clinging to a vine. She automatically pinched her left forearm, but the vision persisted. The vapor-like wraith ran toward Jacob, wobbling as he ran. He reached Jacob and placed both hands on his shoulders as Sarah began the low moans that stuck in her throat.

She saw her son slump forward as the wraith grasped his shoulders. He dragged Jacob backward away from the cliff before disappearing over the cliff himself. Sarah held her breath until the wraith reappeared with Shep in his arms. He placed the frightened pup on the ground. The dog ran to his master and began licking his face as Jacob struggled to push himself to a sitting position. He grabbed his pup as the wraith waited a few feet away. The vision faded, and Sarah rubbed her arm, which was now smarting from the pinches.

There was a sense of peace and closure in Sarah's heart as she began to prepare supper for her son. She did not wait to see if he would be bringing fish home with him. The walk from the river usually took over an hour. Jacob had not been to the cliff before, so she needed to allow extra time for him to return, Again, she sensed she was not alone but felt comforted by the unseen presence. Sarah thanked God for she believed the complete vision had occurred. She waited patiently for her son to return.

*****

Jacob tried to clear his head as he wiped his wet face. He was sitting on the wet ground with Shep licking his face. The whole scene came rushing back to him as he held his pup tightly to his chest. He spotted his fish and belongings a few feet from him. There were drag marks from his heels to the edge of the cliff. Jacob looked around for his rescuer. A vapor wraith about Jacob's size hovered behind him. He struggled to his feet, picked up his belongings, and tried to get his bearings. The storm had turned to a steady rain, but the canopy of trees and foliage protected them. Jacob walked downstream away from the waterfall with Shep and the wraith following. He thanked the wraith, who did not respond to his efforts.

It was after dark when Sarah heard footsteps outside her door. She ran to the door and flung it open for her son. Before he was inside, she wrapped him in her arms. As she released Jacob, a soft vapor brush by Sarah, rushed to the wraith, and enveloped him in her arms as they both began to dissipate. Everyone was safely home.

Being an avid reader, Gaye Hoots was able to be anyone and travel anywhere for a few hours as literature opened the doors to other cultures and worlds. Gaye was born in Davie County, North Carolina, into a farm family who loved to tell stories. Her father made stories come alive and provided humor that made farm chores less tedious. Gaye's grandfather frequently illustrated life lessons through his tales. Gaye passed down these stories to her children and grandchildren. Her writings come from home and work experiences. She contributes to her local paper regularly and many of her short stories and poems have been published. Gaye's greatest desire is to open the magical door of reading for others.

# Grim Reaping

## S. L. Keller

Hearing the relentless buzz in the lunchroom all week about the horrifying experience Bobby Dale Jones and Mitch Kiker endured last Friday night not only intrigued but also aggravated Jessica to the point of kicking her chair back from the table and marching over to where the two boys sat. Placing both hands on the sticky table and leaning over to be eye to eye with Jones, her voice louder than she had planned, "Do you expect any of us to believe you saw the Grim Reaper at some old church?" It was not clear whether this was a question or a statement of fact, as the lunchroom buzz became a low hum and students began pondering the thought.

"We did." Kiker interrupted, "He was huge and just standing there in a hooded cape at that church close to the cemetery."

As Mitch paused to catch his breath, Jessica did not miss a beat, "Mitch Kiker, you're a fool!" and with that judgement, she returned to her seat, mission accomplished!

Both of the boys sat speechless, watching her return to her seat two tables away, the swinging of her long wavy hair emphasizing the validity of her short but direct speech. Neither of them was inclined to go over and contradict her, but as other boys gathered at their table, Bobby Dale took the lead, "She's just a dumb girl! I know what we saw! My brother has seen it several times, so have Dillon and Teddy!" Each sentence came faster than the last as if his need to authenticate the validity of the experience was running out of time.

Jessica's table filled with "friends", supporting her brave verbal assault on the two boys. She nodded accordingly, knowing they would leave as quickly as they had landed. As predicted, the table emptied, leaving only Jessica and her best friend, Allison, sitting alone. "Now," she began, "maybe we can eat in peace."

Allison nodded in agreement, not being one for a great deal of conversation when she could be overheard.

The two girls ate in silence until the sound of clicking heeltaps, a definite no-no regarding school policy, became an immediate distraction. The clicking stopped right behind Jessica. Butch McCall hovered behind her like a vulture and then leaned in as if to whisper in her ear. Instead of the anticipated subtle threats he was known for, his raspy voice rang out. "What would you know about real scary places, Jess? You are just a dumb, mouthy girl!"

Before she thought it through, Jessica wheeled around in her chair, the seat grazing Butch's knee causing him to wince slightly. Standing up to the red-headed bully was easy because he was not used to anyone doing it, least of all a girl. She felt in control as he took a step back, "I can't begin to tell all the scary places I've been, and if I had been on that road trip last weekend with B.D. and Mitch, I sure wouldn't be whining like a baby on how scared I had been!" The words were barely out of her mouth before she began to regret them, as what came next was swift and to be anticipated.

Butch had regrouped and was ready to retaliate. His voice boomed at her, "Well, Miss Smarty Pants, why don't you put your money where your big mouth is? B. D's brother is going to drive down to Salisbury again tomorrow night. I'm sure he would be glad to chauffeur you and your little friend to see it for yourself if you are so brave!" Jessica gulped hard enough that he saw it, so he continued with passion, "So, Miss Bravery, let's hear it; are you in or won't Mommy and Daddy let you go out after dark?"

He did not budge an inch as his eyes pierced hers, waiting for excuses to come, but Jessica held firm. Her face became like stone, and her voice was just as cold, "Of course I'm in, Butch, as long as you are going too!"

He had not anticipated that challenge but was not about to be bested by a girl. "I'm in, of course, I'm in!" He turned, not allowing her to continue her response, the heeltaps clattering as he returned to the waiting boys at their table.

Jessica sat down in the chair, her legs weakened by the adrenaline that had pushed the intensity of her responses. Now Allison only reinforced the gravity of what she had done, the commitment she had made. "Are you nuts?" Allison whispered. "Your folks aren't going to let you go out in a car with those guys."

Jessica was deep in thought, trying to figure a way out, but anything other than following through with the challenge would mark her forever. "I know Alli," she began, "but, I think there is a way to pull it off. You have to help me." Allison's face immediately became pale at the words. Jess's plans always seemed to entangle her in things better left alone. Shaking her head rather than saying no aloud did not faze Jessica, as she picked up her tray and headed to the exit.

Jessica was already out the lunchroom doors by the time Allison caught up with her. Ignoring Allison's desperate looks, Jessica continued, "If I am sleeping over at your house, and you are sleeping over at Diana's, then no one will know." Allison's desperate look changed to confusion, as Jessica unraveled the tale they would both spin to their parents. "Diana's parents don't care what time we get there. Most of the time they are out late on the weekend anyway, so we will be back before they even get home. Diana will cover for us if your folks or mine decide to call and check up." Allison, being clueless to the workings of such a plan, just grunted. "Even if they wanted to talk to one of us, Diana could always say we were in the shower and then conveniently forgot to tell us because she went to sleep before we were finished." Jessica smiled at Allison like a Cheshire cat, feeling the plan was one of her best. Allison followed her quietly into English class, head down, not wanting to be involved in any further conversation about deceiving her parents or facing some unknown horror.

Classes after lunch were boring at the least, but even more so being English and history. Staying awake had always been a problem for Jessica, but not today. She had little more than eight hours to put her plan into motion and perfecting it kept nodding off out of the question. As the final bell rang and eighth graders overtook younger classmen, besting them for chosen seats on the bus, her fate and the destined trip seemed to be the topic of every conversation. Gayle Thompson offered her a seat, but she passed, settling into one that was empty. As she slid over to the window, Allison passed by on the way to her waiting bus. She glanced up at

Jessica with the worst frown she could construct. Jessica smiled and gave her the call me sign as the bus lurched into gear and slowly crept from its parking space.

"Are you really going through with it?" Melanie Maples inquired, twisting around in her seat to face Jessica.

Even if she had second thoughts, Jessica was not backing out. "Of course, I am," she replied with confidence.

No one had claimed the seat next to Jessica, so setting her book bag on the seat as a warning that no one was welcome did not raise an alarm, but this did not deter Trent Murphy, sitting directly behind her, from indirectly giving a history lesson on the Highway 70 Grim Reaper to an attentive audience. "Last year when Don graduated and got a car, he decided to check out the Reaper story and drove out Highway 70, east of Statesville. He had taken some girl to a movie at Newtowne Cinema, and Mom wanted him to pick up something at Kings. She wouldn't be mad if he came in late, so he thought he had plenty of time, and he wanted to impress that girl."

"A girl went?" broke in Kevin Hartsell, "I never heard of a girl going to see it! Who was she?"

Shaking his head, Trent continued, but with his voice lower, "I don't know. She was from Claremont, I think. Don was upset. They had eaten at Village Inn before the movie and still had sodas and popcorn at the show. The only thing he would tell me was that I needed to cover for him Saturday morning so he could get his car detailed, inside and out, once again. He didn't want Mom and Dad to know why he had been more than late or asking questions about the puke all over the car!" Trent drew in a long breath, shaking his head no to the invisible person in Jessica's seat, and then leaned over the seat and whispered in her left ear. "He never saw her again, couldn't get her on the phone, even went to her house and found it gutted by fire."

"It got her!" Kevin interrupted with a validating voice, "Did she kill her family, or did they die in the fire?"

"No," Trent continued, "their neighbor told him they all got out. For some reason, the family did not want to live in Statesville anymore and moved to Wilmington. Don was very different after that. He told me under no circumstances was I to go hunting for the

Highway 70 Reaper. He said the Reaper waits from sunset to dawn every day in front of an old church, close to a cemetery. The Reaper is trying to catch souls before they have a chance to get to heaven, and he will even take them while they are living!" Several gasps were heard from back of the bus, and the constant lurching stops and starts seemed to accentuate the story. "Don said it appears quickly and is looking straight at the road. If you look at him more than two seconds, he gets you, and then it gets foggy, and you are gone."

Jessica felt like she was going to throw up while listening to Trent recount another tale of horror, to which she put more credibility than that of B.J. and Mitch. They were just mouthy seventh-grade boys, she pondered. A frog croaking would scare them. However, Don Murphy was a different story. He just was not the type to make up something like this, and she had heard bits and pieces about the Reaper since sixth-grade. Living an hour away from whatever it was seemed relatively safe, as the thing was only seen at some church, and she had only been to Salisbury a few times with her parents, but it was always during the day. Her Mom loved to shop at Guyes, a very nice women's store, and they would always eat at a great barbeque place on Highway 70 called Hendrix. Other than that, she knew very little about Salisbury or Highway 70 for that matter.

Her thoughts were quickly interrupted as the bus driver almost missed Jessica's stop. Her book bag went sliding off the seat, hurling books up the aisle just as the bus came to a complete stop. Gathering them as quickly as she could amidst words of encouragement, or discouragement, the last thing she heard was Carlene Harwell's lament to the remaining students, "If she doesn't make it, I will miss her." Jessica looked back from the doorway as the driver tried to close the door. Taking another step, Jessica felt she was being abandoned by the roadside as the door slammed shut and the bus again lurched into gear. She stood there looking at faces peering at her, some sympathetic, some smiling. As the bus picked up speed, she saw only the boys pushed to the back windows, all giving her the thumbs down sign, indicating definite failure. They were all boys from her class, but then she realized there was one, glasses thick as Coke bottles, pressing his hand flat against the window as if he would grab her away from this awful thing she had committed to do.

Hurrying away from the bus stop, it was only minutes until she reached home and ran up the steps, meeting her mother coming out the door. "Oh Mom, I'm glad I caught you," she began, even though she was not prepared for this encounter. "Can I sleep over at Alli's tonight? We have so much left to do on our project, and I think it might have a chance at the Science Fair." She was going to continue with some gibberish but was interrupted.

Dressed in her Sunday best, Jessica's mom searched the purse frantically. Jessica had not noticed the two suitcases sitting beside the front door. Finding the keys, and taking a suitcase in each hand, she talked as she walked. "Jess, Daddy's mother is very sick, and we have to go to Pollocksville. I'm picking him up from work and we are driving down. I hope that we can get there before it gets too dark. I just do not like being on country roads at night. It is always so dark, and I feel like something might happen. Oh, how silly, listen to me? You know, I just do not like to be out at night. Is it okay with Alli's mother?"

Jessica grabbed the opportunity immediately, "Sure Mom, she wouldn't have invited me before asking her!"

"Fine then," Mrs. Monroe continued, sounding relieved, "I will call you tomorrow, probably after lunch. If you are not here, I will call Alli's."

Watching her mother sprinting around the car without another word left Jessica with a feeling of accomplishment, having pulled off the scam without batting an eye, but again she felt abandoned, this time by her mother. Going back up the steps and through the front door, the older house seemed to be quieter than usual, even the crack and pop board in the hallway that her father had not gotten around to replacing, was unusually silent. Grabbing the phone, she dialed Alli's number as fast as her fingers would go. The phone rang and rang. Alli was not picking up the receiver! Now what? She knew things were going too smoothly. Before making any further plans and telling any more lies, she looked up B.D.'s number to see if Don was going on another road trip soon. The phone rang only twice before she heard the depth of the voice, which could only belong to Don. At first, she hesitated. Then, "Don? Hi! This is Jess Monroe. I was wondering..."

Don quickly cut in, "Oh, hello Jess! I hear you are going to be our next victim?"

Jessica was in no mood for humor, as this plan might have to change if Alli did not answer soon. "Well, I don't know about the victim part Don, but B.D. and his little friends have been making fools of themselves at school with all this made up nonsense."

Chuckling, Don attempted a more serious tone, "Jess, it isn't nonsense. It isn't some kind of prank. The thing, or whatever you want to call it, is there. That is why I keep going back. You can only look at it for a second or you can be in big trouble. The church is very, very old. It was built in the 1800s, I was told. Highway 70 was only a dirt road back then. People say that thing showed up some time after the church was built. Guess you heard about Willa?"

Jessica was oblivious to the referral and said, "No."

As he continued, Don's voice changed, and she sensed some kind of sadness. "Something happened, Jess. I do not know what, and I tried for months to find out. I really, really liked her, and I thought she liked me, but then I took her to the church. When we came up on it, I quickly looked and then looked back at the road. All I heard her say was, 'He's...' and then she started throwing up. I ran off the road just past the church and grazed a mailbox. She was throwing up and telling me to "Go. Go! GO!" at the same time. There is a back road I can take that connects to Highway 70, so I did not have to pass that church twice in one night. I went that way. She was even throwing up out the window as I was driving. Vomit was everywhere, in the car, on the outside of the car, and it stunk like crazy!" Jess, something happened to her. I think she looked at the Reaper too long and something got hold of her. She never answered any of my calls. For some reason, her family just up and moved far away. I am very serious about this, so if you think this is just a game, I cannot let you go along."

Realizing her quick tongue might get her removed from the road trip, and this was not an option to save her reputation at school, she apologized. "I'm sorry Don. It's just all the BS going around school since last weekend. I am really up for this, and I will do whatever you say. Just bring me back."

Again, she realized her quickness and wit may have caused her to trip over her own tongue, but Don did not reprimand her in any way.

"Where shall I pick you up, Jess?" he asked matter-of-factly.

"My house." As she had the house to herself, picking her up at home was realistic and simple.

"Is it going to be just you or is that Alli girl going too?"

Not knowing where Alli was currently, or why she was not answering the phone, was becoming more distressing to Jessica, but she did not let on in responding to Don's question. "I'm not sure yet. Her folks may not let her go out tonight, Don." He seemed not to care one way or other and confirmed picking Jessica up at eight pm. It would be completely dark when they got to the church to see the Reaper if there were anything to be seen at all.

After dialing Alli repeatedly as she changed into clothes suitable for ghosting or maybe it was reaping, Jessica came to the realization Alli had bailed on her. The easiest thing to do, effectively avoiding the impending road trip, was to ignore the phone. Any other time, Jessica would have walked the four plus miles to Alli's house and had a confrontation at her front door, but this evening was an exception.

Deciding on which clothing was appropriate to dispel a myth or die trying proved more difficult than she imagined. She wanted to look more grown up, but a loose-fitting red sweater and her fat black pants won out. Running might be on the menu tonight, and falling down in the process due to clothes that were too tight made no sense at all. She flipped her hair into a non-descript ponytail and slid into a pair of comfortable lace up tennis shoes, tying and retying them to assure their snugness wound remain with unexpected movement

Just as she saw the last of the sun reflect off the newly detailed Buick Wildcat, it was in her driveway, and she heard that quick staccato horn tap, saying "We're here, where are you?" Jessica headed out the door but as she put her hand on the doorjamb, the feeling she had forgotten something very important overwhelmed her. She was sure Don and whoever else was on the ride would figure she was having second guesses about going, but this was different. She remembered what it was, Daddy's penknife in the key bowl by the door. It was the only weapon she could think of that was small enough for her to hide but sharp enough when stuck in the right place; this Mr. Reaper might not be so scary after all.

Getting to the car, Jess recognized B.D. and Mitch in the back seat alongside Butch McCall. "You get the honor of shotgun," B.D. hollered out, and all three boys laughed as if some great secret were about to be revealed. The door of the '64 Buick Wildcat felt like she was moving a refrigerator. They were really big doors, but so was the whole car. It looked almost like a small yacht. She loved to see Don drive it up the road in front of her house. She could always tell it was Miss Kitty, as Don had fondly named her. When Kitty emerged around the curve onto the long descending hill, the car seemed to float over the pavement, wheels rolling on an invisible ribbon of air. Sliding into the comfortable leather seat, she noted it seemed to be getting dark a little earlier than usual.

Riding shotgun from just outside Newton-Conover to Statesville proved very boring as the conversation centered on Miss Kitty. Don had worked two part-time jobs after school, weekends and summers, saving every penny. He wanted a Buick Wildcat, nothing less. "It's supposed to be the next best thing to owning a Riviera. With a 425 motor and weighing 4,500 pounds, the weight gives her better performance. It's the suspension. They added a link stabilizer bar and a semi-floating rear axle that uses a three-bar link with a track bar."

Jessica did recognize the word floating and interjected, "Is that why it feels like riding in a boat and I am getting seasick?" The boys howled with laughter as Don acknowledged she was right about the floating sensation. The four-door sedan Model 4669, burgundy with black leather interior was beginning to feel like a big coffin, and she was trapped inside with four hyenas. "Just shut up you!" she glared back at Butch, and everyone became silent as Miss Kitty reached the east side of Statesville and floated along the ribbon road, which was as black as the night had become.

About ten minutes after they passed a VFW post, complete with helicopter marking the entrance, Butch spoke up, no humor in his voice, "How far, Don?"

Jessica turned toward Don, noting the cockpit of lights from the dashboard illuminated his face in an eerie sort of way. "Fifteen, twenty minutes maybe. There is a stretch that gets foggy sometimes. Once we get to that point, I will know a little better. This road is in the middle of nowhere, so unless you want to visit with some cows, you probably aren't going to see many cars. Watch for a big plant on the right side of the road. It lights up the sky at night. Weird looking, just pops up out here in the middle of the dark."

B.D. finally spoke up, "What do you think they are making, Don?" Jessica thought B.D. had been sleeping due to his silence, but now realized he had either been listening to the conversation or worrying about what was ahead.

"Not, sure," Don continued, "I heard Dad talking to Mom about it. They were advertising for workers in our paper! He said they must have been looking for a thousand people to advertise so far out. He said they make some kind of fiber."

Don slowed the car, which became swallowed in silence as a thick fog descended. Jessica's earlier feeling of being a bobbing cork quickly left her, but not so much the nausea, which seem more pronounced. "Ten minutes maybe," Don commented. Jessica heard someone in back draw a very loud breath, assuming it was Butch. No one spoke and she was glad. For some unknown reason, she pushed down the lock for the door, putting extra pressure on it with her left pointer finger as it might secure it even deeper in the little home.

Evidently Butch had regained his composure for he noticed her meager attempt at safety and quipped, "Think that's gonna keep out the Reaper Jess?"

B.D. and Mitch chuckled as Jessica responded, "Shut up Butch!"

Jessica wished Don would slow down. Miss Kitty was leaping forward at an urgent pace, as if she were hurrying to get somewhere or trying to get away from something. In the distance, a glow appeared in the sky on the passenger side. The plant, she thought. It rose out of the dark, massive, with lights everywhere. The fog had lifted somewhat, but the mist that lingered gave the lighting a spooky kind of glow, which to her was not very welcoming if they ran into trouble.

"Not far, now" Don interrupted the silence that had returned. No one spoke. Jessica felt her heart pounding in anticipation, and over the next several minutes realized that she was periodically holding her breath. "When the road begins a long curve to the right, you will know that's it. Keep your eyes open. Don't let it sneak up on you. As soon as you see it, look away. Do not, and I mean do not, stare at it! Willa did, and I think it got in her."

Jess had no intention of staring at something that was intent on harming her, but she was determined at least to know what she was looking at. Just as the road began its long curve to the right, the fog came upon them. It was as if you flipped a switch. One second there was the road and then the road disappeared in a cloud of white. Don slowed Kitty to an uncomfortable pace as all eyes scanned the right side of the oncoming landscape, not wanting to be taken by surprise.

"There," was all Don said and the gasp from the back seat was in unison, Jessica, however, did not utter a sound. Rising from the heavy mist, towering 15-20 feet high, there clearly stood something, a hooded cloak falling from massive shoulders, shrouding the unseen face. It seemed to be emerging from the wall of the old church, adjacent to a very old cemetery.

"Go. Go. GO!" Butch screamed with such a high-pitched tone, it could have been Alli instead of him in the back seat. B.D. reached up and grasped Don on the shoulder, "Faster, Don, please," he pleaded. Trying to maintain safety in the fog versus what might await them at the church became a non-issue for Don, as he pressed the car forward. Kitty lurched and with it, Jessica felt her stomach do the same. Grasping at the power window button, Jessica let the window all the way down. Butch was screaming even louder now, "What are you doing Jessica, you want to let it in here?"

She heard another screaming voice but did not recognize it. "I'm trying to let it out!" The voice was hers.

As Miss Kitty sailed through the blackness of the night with no further fog encounter, the tension in the car lessened, and the boys began recounting the horror of seeing the reaper again, while Butch could not finish one sentence without at least one profane word. Don drove silently, Jessica realizing he was looking over at her repeatedly. She did not react, as it was taking every ounce of strength possible to force the contents of her stomach back into place.

Finally, Don whispered, as to not alert the back-seat ghost hunter convention, "Jess? You ok?" She nodded affirmatively but did not speak. The boys were too busy high fiving each other that they seemed oblivious to the reason for coming out tonight and that Jessica had weathered the challenge.

Don drove straight back to Conover. Jessica finally asked him to hurry, noting she wanted to get home in case her mom called, which was a lie. She only wanted to get off Highway 70 as soon as possible. Something was following her. She felt it. Eventually, Don turned onto her street and slowed to a stop in front of her house. Quickly getting out of the car, he went around and opened the door for her, which she did not recognize as being something more than courtesy. Her eyes focused on the dark house. She had forgotten to leave the lights on.

"Jess. Jess?" Don's voice broke through the fog that now seemed to wrap around her.

"Huh" she managed weakly.

"Are you sure you're okay?" he inquired.

"Yeah, yeah." She tried her best at sounding confident.

"Do you want me to walk you up?" he continued.

"No, I'm fine!" she assured him. Realizing she could not walk away from the car without addressing her nemesis in the back seat. "You sleep good tonight, Butch. I think you're the whiney girl!" With that, she turned and quickly ran up the walkway. If she had to say one more word, her stomach was going to revolt, and she was not going to give those boys the satisfaction of seeing her throw up.

Fumbling her key into the door and then trying to find the light switch only intensified her need for a bathroom. Dropping the keys and her purse on the floor, she fled to the closest sink, the kitchen, and began hurling what seemed to be gallons of vomit onto the white porcelain. When the volcanic eruption of her stomach subsided and she had rinsed the sink, her legs would hold her no more, and she sank to the floor, her back against the cabinets. She sobbed. Still shaken from the horrifying experience and weakened from vomiting, she decided to lie on the cold tile floor, not intending to fall asleep and not remembering the front door remained open.

*****

She never heard her father's paper hit the front porch early Sunday morning, as the house stood shrouded in darkness, silent, like a monument to what had gone before. On the other side of town, Don lay awake in the pre-dawn hours, just as he had done Saturday morning, feeling even more unsettled by the Friday night venture down Highway 70. He decided, immediately, it was the last trip, the last time. They had all made it back okay; Jess had not gotten sick and neither had the guys. He was glad to be through with it. Getting up and going in to the kitchen for a glass of water, the Sunday morning paper early edition lay on the table. He retrieved a clean glass from the cabinet, ran his water and started to return to bed, hoping to get some sleep. He casually glanced at the unfolded paper as he passed the table. Suddenly, the glass of water shattered on the floor as the bold headline hit him like a big rock! **LOCAL GIRL DIES TRAGICALLY IN HOME FIRE - Parents Out of Town – Cause Presently Unknown.**

Growing up as a preacher's daughter in rural North Carolina did not lend itself to a very exciting childhood, but at an early age, discovering a gateway that opened on any path imaginable, S. L. Keller's passion for reading skyrocketed. As dreams came alive in the pages of books, she put pen to paper, capturing thoughts in poetry and prose. Thoughts turned to ideas and ideas into stories. An unanticipated early retirement as a registered nurse opened the door for her to pursue her passion for the arts, both literary and visual. Writing now in all genres, from creative non-fiction to her current project, a medical suspense novel, she strives for each story to leave the reader catching their breath and wanting more. S. L.'s website penpaperandbs.com exemplifies her ability to tackle any subject and take the reader on a memorable journey.

# Grim Reaping

## **Advice from 129 Years Ago**

Marie Craig

"Don't forget to pick me up just as soon as school is out today. I don't want to be late for the camping trip." Bruce had already put his pack, sleeping bag, and scout handbook into his mother's old car so he'd be ready to go meet the scout troop that Friday afternoon.

He picked up his books and ran out the door to catch the bus to middle school. He was enjoying being in eighth grade this year but dreaded going to high school next year where he'd be in the lowest grade. Bruce was doing well in his studies but was very shy around the other students because his parents were poor, and he didn't have the nice clothes or belongings like the others. His mother had found the sleeping bag and the pack at a second-hand store, and he hoped the boys wouldn't make fun of him on this trip. They lived in Hickory where his dad had a job in a factory. Most of the other dads were doctors or lawyers and had expensive clothes and possessions.

Some of the other scouts were in his classes, and they looked as impatient as he felt. Bruce thought this was the longest day at school ever because he was excited about going on his first camping trip. They were going to stay at Bakers Mountain Park and cook their own supper on a campfire. This would be great fun, he knew.

They would sleep on the ground in the huge scout tent and then cook breakfast the next morning. His leader, Mr. Jacobs, had planned a trip for them to see an old pioneer village about twelve miles away on Saturday, and then they would go home in the late afternoon. This was all Bruce could think about during his classes that Friday.

Finally, the long day was over, and he ran outside the front of the school, jumped into his mother's car to go meet the other scouts. She gave all sorts of advice about being careful and getting a good night's sleep instead of talking all night. They drove to the meeting place, and Bruce was soon in a big van with his camping gear and the other seven boys.

It was only about ten miles to the park, so the drive was short. The boys tumbled out of the van and grabbed their equipment. Mr. Jacobs had them set up camp by putting up the tent and placing their sleeping bags so they could go to bed quickly in the darkness later. The boys were eager to explore the mountain trails and see the waterfalls, so they got their chores finished quickly, and they headed out with their leader to explore the small mountain. Bruce had no idea there was a mountain that close to Hickory. He had wanted to go to some mountainous areas much farther away, but this was a good choice for a quick ride on the first trip. While in the woods, they saw a tall chimney that had once been attached to a pioneer home. Bruce asked what the house had looked like, and Mr. Jacobs said the pioneer village contained many old homes and buildings that had been preserved which would be similar. He said they would all be made of wood because that was the only building material back then. Rocks were used for building chimneys. One boy asked, "Are any of the houses haunted?" Mr. Jacobs said he doubted that, but Bruce got a funny feeling.

Mr. Jacobs had asked them to bring along their scout handbooks on the hike so they could identify trees. When the boys were in a forest of big trees, they stopped to see if anyone could name them. Bruce knew a few trees, but he'd never seen these big ones before. He knew they were oaks but didn't know what kind. Mr. Jacobs had studied this area before and told them that there were 189 acres of chestnut oaks on this mountain. Bruce learned that this kind of tree usually grew on the tops of mountains and could survive on rocky soil. Mr. Jacobs told them that an acre was about the same size as a football field. That made the size easier to understand. Bruce was thinking that Mr. Jacobs either knew a lot of things or he had prepared well before their camping trip. He seemed to enjoy seeing the boys learn new things. He said the chestnut oak leaves looked a lot like the American chestnut tree leaves. One of the boys knew that the chestnut trees were an important part of the ecology of the Eastern United States until a blight had killed all of them.

He also told them that there were many different types of birds which lived on this small mountain. He had found a list on the Internet of 81 different species that birders had identified for that one park. Bruce knew he couldn't name many birds, but maybe he could learn some more. His mother liked to feed the ones near their home. She would enjoy hearing about all the birds. The boys enjoyed hiking up the mountain and learning more about plants and animals. Bruce hoped all the animals were small.

They cooked supper and enjoyed the food because they'd cooked it and also because they'd worked up an appetite hiking. Bruce had helped cook over the open fire and later checked off some requirements for a merit badge in his scout book. The hike they took up the mountain also got marked in his book. He was excited about gaining some more merit badges at the next court of honor. This was going to be easy and fun.

Mr. Jacobs talked to them that night about this section of Catawba County. "It's quite different from Hickory, which is also in the same county. The pioneers here had a hard life of building a home and a community and growing enough food to store for a long winter. We'll learn more about that tomorrow when we tour the old village. This is the part of the county where I was raised on a farm. Do you know what the name of this township is?"

The boys didn't really know what a township was, so Mr. Jacobs explained that each of the hundred counties in North Carolina was divided into sections called townships. He told them that Catawba County had eight townships. "The town of Hickory, where you live, is in Hickory Township. Right now, we're in Jacobs Fork Township, and the village we'll go see tomorrow is also."

One of the boys, thinking he was just too smart, asked, "Mr. Jacobs, is this your township?" All the boys laughed, but their leader laughed with them.

"Actually, the name comes from the river nearby that is named Jacobs Fork. "Fork" means a section of a river. It's named for a pioneer, Jacob Shuford. So, he's not even my relative, but I remember reading that Jacob was born in 1770 and lived at his father's homeplace on the west bank of the South Fork. We'll cross over Jacobs Creek tomorrow on our ride to the village. We might see some people kayaking in the river. I'll point it out to you. It's been a long time since Jacob Shuford lived in this area, but sometimes names stick around for hundreds of years.

"I remember seeing it called that on a map that a local man drew in 1886. I brought a copy of that map along with me, and I'd like you to look at it." Mr. Jacobs went to the van and returned with several large rolled up maps of Catawba County. At the top on the right side of the oldest map it said "Surveyed and Drawn by R.A. Yoder, 1886." The scouts all crowded in so they could see as Mr. Jacobs pointed out the approximate route they'd driven to the mountain. He showed them another map that was a topographic map of the Bakers Mountain Park. The map had lots of lines drawn on it. Mr. Jacobs explained that the lines described how steep the land is. When the lines are close together, the land is very steep. Bruce had never seen so many interesting maps before and wished he knew more about how to use them. His leader told them that they would be studying many maps in the future to learn about the land before they actually went there. One boy asked how Yoder knew how to draw maps in 1886 when there were no airplanes to take him up to look down. The explanation was that Yoder was a surveyor, and they'd be studying the mathematics that let him draw a map accurately. Some of the boys groaned at that word, but Bruce was eager to learn how to use the math that he enjoyed.

The boys hadn't really gained a respect for local history yet. Their history books sometimes seemed boring and not very important. Mr. Jacobs was hoping to change their minds the next day about studying local history. He told them that at one time, Catawba County had actually been part of the county south of them, Lincoln County. Their leader said that almost all counties had been very large but had been sectioned off into smaller counties such as Catawba which was formed in 1842. He asked the scouts if that was before or after the Civil War. A few of them knew that it was before. Mr. Jacobs liked to apply their schooling to things they experienced. He asked how many years it had been since Catawba became a county. Some of the boys were able to do some mental math and came up with the answer of 177 years in the year of 2019. They all decided that was a long time.

It was getting late, so they all went to bed in the big tent. Bruce had never slept outside before, and he was aware of every sound and movement. He lay awake most of the night really uncomfortable on the hard ground and so close to the other boys. He wasn't really afraid but had a strange feeling when he thought about how they were in a tent that wouldn't offer much protection from beasts or bad people. He finally drifted off to sleep about an hour before everybody else was getting up. His legs were sore from the hike up the mountain the day before, and he was really sleepy now.

He made himself get up, and he felt better when he had something to eat. They rolled up the tent, packed all the gear into the van, made sure they'd cleaned up after themselves, and put the campfire out. He'd enjoyed being on this small mountain and thought that he'd like to bring his family here sometime. They drove down the mountain, and Mr. Jacobs stopped to let them see Jacobs Fork on the way to the pioneer village. They got out of the van and walked onto the bridge. There were some kayakers just entering the river. Bruce thought he would like to try that sometime. As he stood watching the water run under the bridge, he felt a little dizzy, but decided it was because he was sleepy and tired.

They drove on a curvy narrow road south and then headed east on another road to go to the village. Bruce wasn't sure he could find the way if he convinced his family to come on this same trip. They had been told that this part of the trip was twelve miles, but it seemed much farther than that to Bruce. He saw a sign when they were headed east that said "Greedy Highway." Mr. Jacobs didn't know why it was called that. He said maybe it was somebody's last name. It was a crooked road that made Bruce's tummy upset, but he willed himself to feel better.

This road ended, and they had to go either north or south on Plateau Road. Mr. Jacobs had studied his maps and reference books before the trip, and he remembered there had been a community named Plateau many years ago, and the name continued to mark the road. He knew to turn south and after several more intersections, the van came to a stop at the pioneer village. Bruce was eager to exit the van and get some fresh air. He was still very sleepy and a little disoriented after the curvy road.

Mr. Jacobs had them gather near him so he could give instructions. "Stay together, boys, and don't wander off. This part of the county doesn't have a lot of residents because of the big agricultural fields and the parks like the one we visited last night. Our host will be here in a few minutes, and I want you to be on your best behavior. These buildings are old, and we don't want to damage them."

"Does anybody live here?" asked one boy.

"No, but all of the homes and outbuildings were part of farms many years ago. Some of them have been moved here and reconstructed." Bruce decided they looked a little spooky; almost like the ghost town they'd toured one summer.

When their host, Max, who was also the owner and manager of this village arrived, he talked to them about the purpose of some of the buildings. There were homes, a church, barns, stores, storage buildings, and even a one-room schoolhouse. They started their tour, and Bruce trudged along with the scouts even though he was tired. This was a special tour just for them, but Max said that sometimes people dressed up like that time period and demonstrated weaving, spinning, milking a cow, and things like that.

The boys were able to enter a few homes and were surprised how small they were and how few things people owned back then. They didn't even have ranges in the kitchen for cooking but had big pots hanging in the fireplace. Bruce began to think that his meager home had more equipment and size than these old buildings. Maybe he wasn't as poor as he had thought.

He enjoyed seeing the barn and the pastures where the cows grazed. He wasn't sure he could get up every morning and go milk cows, though.

They all went into the old school next. It was sure different from the boys' school. The windows were small, and there was a big wood stove in the middle of the room. The boys and Mr. Jacobs sat up front on the school benches so the owner could tell them about the school. Bruce decided he would sit in the very back so that everybody wouldn't see how sleepy he was. He heard the information that the school, Ebenezer School, had been moved there, and they thought it was built in 1840! The boys were amazed at the age of the building. It had two doors so the boys could enter one door and the girls the other door. That's all Bruce heard before he lay down on the bench to rest for a minute. Nobody would see that he wasn't listening.

Bruce thought he would just close his eyes briefly, but he fell fast asleep. The owner, Mr. Jacobs, and the other boys left the schoolroom and went to visit other buildings, not noticing that they were missing one scout.

Bruce was actually dreaming about this village, especially the school, and awoke to see a boy in overalls about his age standing in front of him. Bruce couldn't decide if he were still asleep but then remembered about the people dressing up in old timey clothes. He decided this boy must be one of the team that demonstrated in the old buildings. Sitting up quickly, Bruce was embarrassed to be caught sleeping. The other boy said, "That's ok. I go to sleep sometimes when I'm here." That really confused Bruce.

The boy seemed eager to strike up a conversation and continued, "My name is Nathan Shull. My home is real close by, and I walked over to see who all these people are. We don't get a lot of visitors."

Bruce told the boy his name and asked Nathan how often he dressed up like that. "Shucks, this is how I dress all the time. When you live on a farm and have to work hard, you don't have fancy clothes. My folks are just trying to keep their little farm and home. It's not easy when there are eight people in the same small house."

Bruce told him that he lived in town with his parents, but they didn't have a farm. Bruce told the boy his dad worked in a factory and that they had a hard time paying for everything they needed. Both boys realized they had something in common. Nathan said it didn't bother him much that they were poor – he had his family, enough to eat, and was happy. Bruce realized these were important goals and that he was more fortunate than he'd realized. He then remembered something he'd heard his dad say: "Clothes do not make the man." Instead of feeling sorry for himself, he'd think about all the good things in his life and be grateful for his family. There were several students in his class who had only one parent.

54

He was real lucky to have two parents who really cared for him well. He decided he needed to tell them he appreciated them.

Bruce asked Nathan where he went to school. "I already told you that this is my school right here." Even though Bruce remembered that, he still didn't understand. He then asked Nathan how many students went there. Nathan said it depended on the weather and what season it was. "During the fall we have to stay home and put up the crops for the winter."

Bruce asked, "Don't you get in trouble for not going to school? We have to go 180 days, and if we miss too often, our parents get an email from the school."

Nathan looked at him in confusion and asked, "What's an email? I never heard of that." Bruce told him it was a message on a computer or a phone. Nathan looked even more perplexed. "How does it work?" Bruce said he couldn't really explain it, but the words went through the air and ended up on a computer. "What's a computer?" Bruce was beginning to get a little annoyed and wondered if this boy was playing a trick on him.

Bruce asked him, "Who's the President of the United States?"

"Benjamin Harrison, of course. Our teacher makes us learn important things like that. Don't you know who the President is?" Bruce didn't know exactly what year Harrison served, but he knew it was a long time ago.

Bruce said, "You sure are good at pretending to be a long ago student. You're doing a good job." When he said this, Nathan got angry and told him that he wasn't pretending anything. "This is 1890, and nothing you say will make me realize it's not. What year do you say it is?"

This astonished Bruce, and he quickly said, "This year is 2019. If I had my calendar with me, I'd show you. I'd rather talk about things we can agree on. Where do you sit in this classroom?"

Nathan laughed and said, "Certainly not on this side — this is the side the girls sit on!" Bruce remembered hearing that the doors were separate but didn't realize the classroom was the same way. Bruce told him that the boys and girls in his school could sit next to each other. Nathan said he wished it was like that for him. Bruce asked who cooked lunch for them at school. Nathan told him that he brought a dinner pail with a biscuit and a cooked potato every day. Bruce told him about their large cafeteria with hot food and sometimes pizza. Nathan didn't know what a pizza was, so Bruce had to describe it to him. Bruce told him how much lunch cost each day, and Nathan said that was so much money that he couldn't believe it.

Nathan said his teacher was pretty old and had served in the Civil War and told them about his experiences. "Man, I'd love to hear that; we don't talk much about war and there's nobody left who served in that war," said Bruce. He couldn't imagine that he was actually believing that Nathan was from another time period – 129 years ago! This can't be happening, he thought. He decided he needed some proof from Nathan and tried to figure out a way to make others believe that this had really occurred.

Bruce finally thought of a plan. "I found a penny up at our campground last night on the mountain and put it in my pocket for good luck. If you have a penny, we could swap." Nathan fished around in his pocket for a minute and finally produced a penny. When Nathan showed the back side to Bruce, he couldn't tell that it was old, but when Bruce turned it over and saw the side of a man's head with a feather headdress and the numbers 1890 below the head, he realized this was an old coin. The band on the headdress said *Liberty*. Bruce didn't know much about value, but when they had exchanged coins, he realized he now had something very special. He wondered how Nathan would explain the coin of the future to his family and friends.

"What do you do on your farm to help?"

"I have to get up early every morning and milk our cow so we have enough milk to feed everybody. At harvest time, I help in the fields, pulling corn and picking beans. We also grow a lot of other vegetables that my mother cans."

"My mother used to talk about canning. She works at home sewing for people, so she doesn't have time to can anymore. She just buys food at the grocery store."

The boys each realized that they needed to end their visit and go their separate ways but were reluctant to do so.

"I'm going to have to go back home now. My folks will wonder where I've been for so long. I need to help Ma hang out clothes to dry so that we'll have clean things to wear to church tomorrow. It's been good talking to you, Bruce. I doubt we'll ever see each other again, but I won't forget you. I probably won't say anything to my family about this meeting with you. I don't think they'd believe me. I'll keep this penny in a safe place where nobody will find it. Good luck with your schooling and your future. Remember to help other people and not think about yourself."

Bruce was sad to see Nathan leave. He realized that some things never change through the years – friendship, self-image, and hope for a happy future. He said, "Best wishes for a happy future for you, too." He had tears in his eyes as he said it, and when he turned around Nathan was gone. Bruce ran out the door to look for him, but there was no sign of Nathan.

He took a deep breath to steady himself and decided to go look for the other scouts. Bruce closed the schoolhouse doors and started walking through the village. He found his friends coming out of the old church. They all realized that Bruce hadn't been with them for a long time. They said, "Where've you been?"

Bruce decided not to tell about meeting Nathan. That would be his own special memory and learning experience. He put his hand in his pocket and felt the 1890 penny to reassure himself that it actually had happened. When he joined his friends, he was more talkative and interested in what they had to say instead of being so shy and unsure of himself. "I was doing an in-depth study of the old school and its students," he told them.

~~~~~

*Marie chose to honor Boy Scouts because her husband, two sons, and five grandsons all excelled in Boy Scouts.*

~~~~~

Marie Craig was a teacher of math but is now a teacher of genealogy and tatting. In addition to editing genealogical newsletters, she is webmaster for five genealogical sites. She has written six books about Davie County history, focusing on military service, schools, and first responder service within the county. She received the North Carolina Genealogical Society Award, the North Carolina Society of Historians Award, the Willie Parker Peace Award, and the President's Award from North Carolina Society of Historians. Her goal is to write children's books that use her knowledge of Davie history to teach young people about local history. Marie also enjoys playing the piano and organ and directing the Davie County Singing Seniors.
Website: http://sites.google.com/view/booksbymariecraig/home.

# Arabella's Ashes

N. R. Tucker

"Don't you know the story?" Zacharias let the way down the path to Hunting Creek.

Hazel rolled her eyes. "Everyone knows the Hall homestead burned in a fire. The whole family died."

"And the shade?"

"There's no such thing." Hazel's eyes cut to Sophronia for confirmation.

"It's just a story." Ignoring the creaks and groans, Sophronia crossed the old bridge over the creek. No longer stable enough for a horse and cart, the kids could still cross one at a time.

Rebeka winked at Zacharias. "I wish to hear the tale, if only to be sure the telling is true."

Zacharias crossed the bridge and reached back to steady Rebeka's step onto land. "Many years ago, Phineas Hall moved his family from Morganton to Hunting Creek. He built his homestead between the fork of the creek with running water on three sides of his land. Phineas was a mean old man. He couldn't abide strangers and shot at anyone who passed near his land. Soon, even travelers knew to stay away. There were whispers of strange occurrences near the homestead. Small animals, killed, but not eaten. Peculiar sounds, especially at night."

The kids passed the burnt remains of the homestead, and Zacharias lowered his voice. "During the October full moon, with All Hallows Eve approaching, Phineas became moonstruck. He took his hunting knife, stabbed his sons, and then his wife, leaving Arabella, his only daughter, for last. When Phineas saw what he had done, he burned down the house while he was still inside. They say he never left, and his shade guards the burnt ruins, making sure no one settles here. On a full moon, his cries of anguish as he burns echo through the valley."

Hazel heard movement in the bushes and jumped. It was only a covey of bobwhites. "Why are Cora and Augustus building here?" If she were getting married, she wouldn't want to live near haunted land.

"Father gifted them the land on this side of the creek, south of the Hall homestead. Where else would they build?" Sophronia asked.

Hazel's eyes darted around the clearing. Nothing unusual. Twilight wouldn't be for hours. Even so, the trees, without their leaves, took on the appearance of arms with long gnarled fingers. Her hands trembled, but Hazel said nothing. She wouldn't give Zacharias another reason to tease her. He was never mean on purpose, but he was fond of pranks. Her father called Zacharias a trickster. Hazel glanced at Jared, Zacharias's twin. Jared was kind.

Jared sighed. "That poor family. Why was his heart filled with such evil?"

Edmund clapped his hands together. "Enough stories. We promised we would clear the brush for Augustus and Cora."

Zacharias plopped down under a tree and stretched out. "We have all afternoon."

"If we haven't completed the task this day, Father will not be pleased. I was allowed to come to work, not tell tales." Sophronia ushered the others toward the stakes.

Everyone, even Zacharias, worked. Sophronia and the girls pulled vines and weeds. The boys dug up the larger bushes. They worked the rest of the day, roasting in the unseasonable heat of fall. The humidity was, unfortunately, at its normal high for the season.

The sun began its descent behind the mountains, adding red and orange tones to the sky. Even though it was warm, Hazel shivered. "We must leave. I don't want to walk home in the dark."

Zacharias chuckled. "Are you afraid Phineas will show up?"

"No." Hazel's eyes scanned the landscape.

Moving closer to Hazel, Zacharias whispered, "Tonight's an October full moon. Just like the night Phineas killed his family."

Jared glared at his brother. "Enough." Turning to Hazel, Jared said, "Don't worry. It's just a story. Shades aren't real."

A giggle floated through the air. Everyone turned toward the sound, but all they saw were the deepening shadows of twilight on the landscape.

"What was that?" Hazel moved closer to Jared.

"Naomi," Zacharias yelled. "I told you not to follow us." Zacharias ran down the path into the trees toward the giggle he thought was his youngest sister. Naomi was forever following Jared and him when they left the farm. She was too young to cross the creek alone.

Edmund matched Zacharias's pace, and together, they rounded a huge boulder where the path became an open field. A thick mist rolled toward them. Zacharias looked up. His eyes widened, and his mouth dropped open. Shaking, Zacharias grabbed Edmund's arm and pointed toward the edge of the clearing where the mist originated. A girl about their age floated above the ground. The trees and shrubs behind her were visible through her transparent form.

The shade waved.

Their screams broke the silence.

Hazel, last to round the large rock, was also the last to see the shade. She gripped Jared's arm and gasped. No coherent words escaped her lips.

Jared tightened his hold on Hazel and ran back the way they had come, leading the kids back to the clearing where they had worked all afternoon. Hazel stopped abruptly, and Jared stumbled. He followed Hazel's horrified gaze. The shade floated before them with her hair and skirt blowing though there was no wind.

Zacharias and Rebeka, the last to reach the clearing, were the first to turn and run to the bridge. The others were close behind.

The shade giggled again and appeared in front of the bridge, blocking Zacharias and Rebeka from crossing the water.

Gasping for breath, and realizing they couldn't outrun the shade, Zacharias asked, "Are you... Arabella?"

"Yes, I'm Arabella Hall. I heard what Jared said about Father. He's right. Evil does lurk in Father's heart."

"He's here?" Hazel squeaked and peered into the shadows of twilight. She saw nothing.

"Of course. Father trapped me here."

"Why?" Jared stepped between Hazel and Arabella. His hand accidently passed through Arabella. The cold chilled him to the bone.

"You shouldn't do that. I don't mind, but the living always complains of cold when they pass through my body even if they can't see me." Arabella smiled mischievously.

"How do you know... never mind." Jared rubbed his numb digits together and changed his question. "How did he trap you?"

"I don't know. But he did. Mother isn't here, and neither are my brothers. It's just me and Father."

"That's awful," Hazel said, peeking out from behind Jared. Arabella nodded.

"Is he confined to the burned house?" Sophronia asked.

Arabella shook her head. "If I can travel here, he can. I heard you speak of a couple building their home on this side of the creek. Finally, I shall have someone to visit. I'm so lonely."

"Cora won't welcome a shade," Sophronia said.

"Neither will Augustus." Hazel nodded her agreement.

Arabella looked hopefully between the teenagers. "If you were to banish Father, he would be gone, and I would be free. Perhaps I could join Mother and my brothers. Then there would be no spirits here."

"How could we do that?" Jared asked.

63

Surprise flickered across Arabella's face, and she stared at Sophronia. "Cast a banishing spell."

Hazel shook her head. "We aren't witches to know such things."

Sophronia pursed her lips. "How can we be sure you speak the truth?"

"I suppose my plight is hard for the living to understand." Arabella pouted.

Still rubbing his cold fingers, Jared stood before the floating form. "Tell us more. What happened before the fire?"

Arabella nodded solemnly. "One day, Father told Mother to pack. We moved from Morgansborough to here. Eventually, I tired of only seeing my family. Father would not allow anyone to visit, and only he made trips into town. One by one, my brothers left, never to return. I begged to go back to town. I missed everyone."

"Did your brothers really leave?" Zacharias asked.

Arabella's eyes narrowed on Zacharias. A single tear rolled down her cheek. The light from the rising moon made the tear shine. "I don't know. Do you think Father killed them like he did me? If so, why aren't they here?"

Jared said, "I don't know, but we'll help."

"We aren't witches," Hazel said, repeating her earlier comment.

"We'll think of something." Jared's confidence made Arabella smile.

"Please help me. I'll be ever so grateful." Arabella vanished in the mist.

As they crossed the bridge, Zacharias nudged his brother. "If Papa finds out you're helping a shade, he'll confine you to our house for all eternity."

*****

"Child, what has you so gloomy?" Mama Flora continued to knead the bread.

Sophronia added fresh vegetables to the stew over the hearth before she spoke. "Did you know there are two shades at the Hall homestead?"

Mama Flora stopped kneading the bread and looked at Sophronia. "What happened?"

"Yesterday, as we cleared the land for Cora and Augustus, we met Arabella Hall, a shade." She paused, hoping her grandmother would say something. Mama Flora didn't speak, so Sophronia added, "Arabella said her father, also a shade, keeps her captive. She wants our help to banish him, so she can join her mother and brothers in the afterlife."

"Banishing a shade is no small thing." Mama Flora returned to kneading the bread.

"Did you know they were there? Does Cora?"

"I know nothing. Just rumors. And Cora doesn't have the gift. Are you sure Arabella is the one who needs saving?"

"She said –"

"Child." Mama Flora talked right over Sophronia. "Shades don't change their personalities at death. Some are good, some bad. You better know the difference before you agree to help one. Mama Cornelia always said, 'In avoiding one evil, care must be taken not to fall into another.' You would do well to remember that."

"What does that mean?"

Boots stomped up the outside steps. Mama Flora shook her head. "Mind the stew. This is not a subject for the entire family."

Sophronia sighed. The only one of four siblings to have the gift, she had not been trained. Her father, Rufus, came from witch blood, but Sarah, her mother, didn't. Not realizing she had married into a witch family, Sarah had gone about the business of farming and raising children with her husband.

At the age of four, Sophronia called magic for the first time. Wanting the cookie Cora, her elder sister, had yet to eat, Sophronia reached out her hand, and the cookie floated into it. Laughing, she stuffed the prize in her mouth before Cora could retrieve it. Three years older than Sophronia, Cora had complained over the loss of her cookie. Mama Flora realized what had happened, and Sophronia's training started immediately. That wasn't enough for Mama. Citing her fear for Sophronia's life if the neighbors learned of Sophronia's magic, Sarah begged Mama Flora not to train Sophronia, but instead to teach her to ignore her abilities.

When Sophronia was ten, she had promised Mama, on her deathbed, to stay away from magic. Sophronia had kept that promise for four years. Perhaps that was a mistake. Had she studied, she might already know about shades. Turning back to the stew, Sophronia wondered what Mama Flora had yet to tell her.

Jared did his own research by asking his father if he believed in shades. His father, a farmer who studied the Bible and preached a sermon each Sunday for the families who lived near Hunting Creek, was vocal on the subject. "Any spirit that is not of God, is a demon, therefore, evil. Do not seek them out. God forbids communicating with the dead. Now tell me boy, what is your interest?"

"Curiosity. The shade of the Hall homestead was discussed while we cleared the land for Augustus and Cora."

"I suppose you mean Zacharias tried to scare the girls?"

"No, Papa. We were just talking."

"As you say. It's time for you to milk the cow."

"Yes, Papa." Jared made a hasty retreat, glad he wasn't in trouble. Hopefully, his question didn't get Zacharias in trouble.

*****

"You sure this is a good idea?" Sophronia asked. Once again, they headed across the old bridge to the Hall homestead, this time to search for clues about the Hall family. An early morning fog covered the ground, but the sun would soon fix that. Sophronia used to love the mist, but now the vapors curling up toward the heavens reminded her of Arabella and the impact it could have on Sophronia's family.

Jared didn't slow down. "Arabella needs our help."

"We better be sure what evil we fight," Sophronia said, remembering what Mama Flora had told her.

Hazel nodded. "Sophronia's right."

"Don't worry, the sun is still high in the sky. No shades today." Zacharias passed the others and led the way to the burnt hull of the homestead.

"Why ever would you say that?' Arabella appeared next to Rebeka.

Rebeka was so startled she slipped and fell through Arabella. Zacharias caught Rebeka and steadied her. Even though it was warm for October, she shivered. Placing his cloak around her, Zacharias glared at Arabella. "How are you here?"

Arabella said, "Where else would I be? I told you I can't cross the water or leave Father's land."

"But... it's daylight."

"Daylight? The sun doesn't bother me. It is harder for someone to see me in the sun, but it's not impossible." Arabella waved her arms around.

"Oh." Zacharias wanted to argue, but the proof floated in front of him. Arabella's translucent figure, decidedly less muted in color but more transparent than in the moonlight, might be easier to ignore, but she was identifiable. "We have a few more questions."

"Do you?" Her eyebrows raised, and she didn't sound welcoming.

Sophronia said, "If you want our help, you need to prove you're not evil."

Anger washed over Arabella's face, but she quickly schooled her features into an understanding smile. "I know your family. The Clarks out of Morgansborough, right? Your great-grandmother told Father to move out here."

Sophronia crossed her arms over her chest. "You're wrong."

Arabella's smile widened. "Mama Cornelia had one child, Flora. Flora married Enoch Clark, and they had a son named Rufus. Isn't he your father?"

Sophronia frowned. How did Arabella know her family? And how much did she know?

Arabella floated around Sophronia in lazy circles. "If you were ailing, you went to Mama Cornelia. Everyone knew that. She told Father if he moved us away from town, things might get better. I heard her."

Jared and the others stared at Sophronia.

Sophronia shrugged. "Mama Flora, like her mama before her, is a midwife and helps others when there's no doc around. You know this since most of you have been helped by Mama Flora at one time or another." Turning to Arabella, Sophronia asked, "How do you know what Mama Cornelia said to your father?"

"I was picking herbs under the open window." Arabella stopped moving and floated in front of Sophronia. "I think Mama Cornelia intended to help. It just didn't work."

"What did Mama Cornelia think would get better by moving?" Sophronia glared at Arabella.

"I'm not sure." Arabella thought for a moment and said, "I suppose she thought Father's anger and strange behavior would improve if he were away from everyone."

"We still don't know how to help," Hazel said.

"There must be a way." Jared removed his hat and scratched his head.

Sophronia felt a chill, and the hair on her arms stood up, followed by an uneasy feeling, and a whiff of burning wood. She looked toward the rocks at the edge of the woods. A thick, dark mist rolled into the clearing and completely hid the rocks. Sophronia asked, "What's that?"

The mist, dark as night, passed the rocks and moved toward them, obscuring everything in its path.

"It's Father. You should leave. Save yourselves." Arabella's normally lightly tinted mist darkened. "Run!"

They didn't. The friends were too busy watching the black mist congeal into the form of a man. A man whose color wasn't muted at all. He wore raggedy clothes. His hair and beard were long and unkept. His disheveled appearance was at odds with Arabella's curled locks and tidy clothes.

"None are welcome here. Pain and death reside on this side of the creek." Phineas's voice, low and rough, weaved around them.

"Let her join her mother," Jared said.

"Fool." Phineas grabbed Arabella. She struggled but was no match for her father. The black mist darkened around the two shades. The mist and shades disappeared.

Jared waved his hands at the empty field. "Now do you believe? We have to help Arabella."

*****

Sophronia walked into the garden where her grandmother selected plants for a poultice. Jared's father had injured his arm, and the compress would pull out the infection.

Mama Flora didn't look up. "Cut two sprigs each of oregano and echinacea. Dig up one bulb of garlic. The mortar and pestle are on that rock. Crush the three together before adding the honey. Then you can walk the poultice over to Mister Turner. You know how to apply it."

Knowing Mama Flora wouldn't talk until the compress was made, Sophronia did as instructed. Task complete, she asked, "Did you know the Halls?"

"Not well. They moved from Morganton, Morgansborough as it was called then."

"Arabella knows a lot about our family."

"You're not still talking to that shade, are you?"

"We saw her father grab her and carry her away. Shouldn't we help?" Sophronia blurted out, "Do you know how to banish a shade?"

Mama Flora didn't look up from her cuttings.

"Do you?"

Taking a deep breath, Mama Flora said, "Yes, I know a banishing spell. If you must continue down this foolish path, there are other things you need to know."

"Am I to be trained?" Sophronia cringed as she spoke. She had promised her mother she wouldn't become a witch, not even a white witch, like her grandmother. She had always been careful to ignore the strange things that happened around her.

"If you must banish a shade, then you must be trained." Mama Flora raised a dirt covered hand and patted Sophronia on the cheek. "Don't look so miserable. There's good in being a witch. You can help people with the potions and spells I teach you, but banishing shades is not for the timid. Who will help you?"

"Won't you?"

"I'll train you, but I can't fight this shade," Mama Flora said. "I knew Phineas Hall. I remember a good man caring for his family as best he could. By that time, I was married to your grandfather, your father had just been born, and we lived across town. I don't know what happened. Mother would never speak of it except to say I shouldn't think badly of Phineas. He was not the monster the town accused him of being. Even now, I trust her judgement and believe in his innocence. I cannot banish him. You must believe banishment is needed for it to work."

"There's only him and Arabella. She must have been about my age when her father killed her. How could she be evil?" Sophronia thought for a few minutes and asked, "What must I do?"

Mama Flora explained, and Sophronia asked, "How will I do all of that?"

Mama Flora smiled. "I'll teach you."

*****

"What are you doing now?" Edmund asked.

"You said you didn't want to know." For over a week, Sophronia had prepared to banish Arabella's father. She didn't look up but continued to sort the crystals according to Mama Flora's instructions.

Jared shook his head. "Tell me again how you know this."

An exaggerated sigh was Sophronia's only response.

"Are you a witch?" Jared ran his fingers through his hair. "I'm not going to tell anyone. It's just that… we're banishing a shade. Seems to me only a witch would know how to do that."

Sophronia blushed but didn't speak.

Edmund dropped down beside her and picked up a thin, smooth stone with stripes layered in the stone like a rainbow, although the colors were shades of brown and orange only. Turning it over in his hand, he said, "We promise not to tell. The others don't have to know." He raised the stone and said, "But you have to explain this."

Sophronia slowly looked up from her task, and a small smile lit her eyes. "It's agate. It drives away spirits, protects from psychic attack, and stops magic."

"Huh?" Edmund was surprised to hear Sophronia discuss such things. She really must be a witch. He thought about that truth for a second and realized he didn't care. She was still his friend. "Do I get one?"

"I made a pouch for you, me, and Jared. It will take three of us to form the circle."

"Circle?"

"To banish a shade. Three is the minimum number. The others won't be needed, but somehow, I need to spread a salt circle and a few other items around all of our homes on the next full moon."

"Salt?" Jared asked.

Edmund's eyes widened. "Full moon?"

"Salt is a purifier, used for cleaning and protection." Sophronia gathered her supplies and stood.

"You'll have to explain all these rules to us if we're to help." Jared picked up a black stone that slipped out of Sophronia's hands. "What's this?"

"Black tourmaline. It repels dark forces," Sophronia said.

Jared returned the stone to the pile. "Good. Once her father is banished, Arabella can join her mother and brothers."

Edmund asked, "How you gonna explain this to your Pa?"

"I'm not. Papa lectured me just for asking about shades. I'll not explain we plan to banish one."

Edmund tossed Jared a disbelieving look. "You don't think your father will notice a salt circle?"

"Hope not." Jared stared back at Edmund. "How about you?"

"Papa always hunts during the full moon. I'll tell Mama I'm spending the night in the barn watching the plow horse, that's sick." The others gawked, and Edmund grinned. "I sleep in the barn sometimes, just to get away from everyone. Mama will know the horse isn't sick, but she won't stop me."

Sophronia finished explaining the cleansing ritual, and both boys frowned.

"We have to do all of that on the full moon?" Jared groaned. "If Papa doesn't catch me, it will be a miracle."

"When we do this, do we become witches?" Edmund asked.

"Banishing a shade isn't witchcraft," Sophronia explained. Deciding to trust her two best friends who she knew had already figured out the truth, she added, "Witches have recorded the instructions, but a shade doesn't need a witch to complete a banish. Anyone who completes the tasks can do it."

"Only a witch would know what to do," Edmund retorted.

*****

It was a sunny November afternoon. Sophronia, Edmund, and Jared sat by the creek on rocks. Rebeka and Hazel watched Zacharias fish. He had bragged he could provide enough fish to feed all four families that evening.

Edmund leaned in and whispered, "Tonight's the full moon. Everything ready?"

"Yes. You both have your supplies hidden," Sophronia said. "Any questions?"

"We've each got our own house, but who's going to protect Hazel's home?" Jared leaned back against a tree.

"I will," Sophronia said.

"Alone?"

"Not alone," Edmund replied.

"Of course, alone. Mama Flora will cover for me if Father notices. I don't even have to sneak out, unlike you."

"She's right," Jared said.

"I don't like it." Edmund skipped a pebble across the water.

"Hey," Zacharias yelled at Edmund for scaring the fish. "It's a good thing I already caught enough."

Edmund felt the heat as a blush rose up his cheeks. "Sorry."

Zacharias tossed the last fish in the basket and walked over to the trio. "What are you three discussing? Whenever you get together, you whisper and stop speaking if anyone is near."

"I thought it was just me," Hazel said. She and Rebeka had followed Zacharias. She looked at Jared and asked, "Did you figure out how to help Arabella?"

"What? No," Jared said.

"You did. I knew it." Zacharias grinned. "You can't lie well at all."

"I think it's admirable that Jared doesn't lie well," Hazel said.

Jared blushed.

"Are we sure we should help Arabella?" Zacharias asked.

"Why shouldn't we?" Sophronia asked. She had been thinking the same thing herself, but she wasn't sure why.

"I don't know, but something's not right. I think Arabella's not telling us the whole truth."

"I think she's scared of her father. That's why she's cautious around us," Rebeka said. Turning to Sophronia, she asked, "What do we need to do?"

Sophronia shook her head. "Nothing."

"Actually, they could help," Edmund said.

Sophronia glared at him.

"Zacharias can be lookout for Jared. Rebeka can be mine. Hazel can be Sophronia's lookout at her house. That way we all have help." Edmund grinned, pleased with his solution.

"Explain," Zacharias said.

Sophronia frowned, not happy with this turn of events. Sophronia finished explaining the tasks at a high level, and Zacharias asked, "Where did you get this information?"

Jared tapped himself on the chest. "Remember when I went to Morganton a couple of weeks ago with Papa? I slipped away to visit Old Lady Walker. She had the information we needed. Mama Flora collects rocks and has plenty of herbs, so Sophronia gathered the ingredients without being caught."

Sophronia shot Jared a look of thanks.

"I'm impressed. Escaping Papa and going to see the one person in town he told us to never approach." Zacharias thumped Jared on the back in approval. He divided up the fish between his friends, and they parted company.

During dinner, Jared's father lectured his children on the evils of disobedience, saying omission was as bad as a lie. Thinking they were found out, Jared and Zacharias squirmed until Papa zeroed in on Dorcas, their older sister. She had been spotted talking to Jeramiah Hayes on more than one occasion. Papa finally told Dorcas to invite the boy to dinner. He didn't object to the boy, but he did object to Dorcas's sneaking.

Everyone went to bed on time except Papa. The girls were in their room, and Mama was asleep in the room she shared with Papa. Jared waited on the upstairs landing where the boys slept, pretending to be asleep. Finally, Papa closed his Bible, climbed the stairs, and blew out the lamp. Once he heard snoring, Jared carefully slipped out.

Earlier in the evening, Jared and Zacharias made a game of playing with a cow bell and rang it in every corner of the house to break up stagnant energy. Jared sprinkled the dried crushed herbs, prepared by Sophronia, around the house. Hopefully, Mama wouldn't sweep behind the furniture in the corners for a few days.

By the light of the moon, Jared walked over to the barn and recovered the pouch of supplies Sophronia had provided. He cleared his stones in the running water of Hunting Creek.

Next, he held each crystal one at a time, dedicating it to its purpose. Two black tourmaline stones and four obsidian were dedicated to protection, the agate to drive away spirits, and the garnet to reinforce the power of the herbs. Following Sophronia's instructions, he placed all but one of the stones around the house, whispering,

"I cleanse my home and self today.
These stones they shall preserve
And not this home or land betray.
Protection it shall serve."

The obsidian he placed on a string around his neck.

The circle of salt was next on his list. Jared started outside the northern corner of the house, walked clockwise, and outlined the perimeter with salt. Sophronia had provided the salt, and he didn't question how she managed it. His mother would certainly miss this much salt. This time Jared whispered,

"I am power, strong in belief.
My work this night will smite.
Through rituals I find relief,
And guard this home from blight."

Tasks complete, Jared sneaked back into the house, crept up the stairs, and crawled back into bed.

Edmund and Sophronia completed the same set of rituals at their homes, although Sophronia had a few more tasks to complete. The one exception was a jade necklace, a powerful talisman for her family that Mama Flora had given her earlier in the day. Though the obsidian would protect against psychic and magical attacks, the jade – according to her grandmother – would deflect the attack back on the sender with three times the power. Too bad they only had one piece of jade, but unlike the other stones, jade did not reside in the mineral-rich mountains nearby.

Once her home was protected, Sophronia took the path to Hazel's. She had never found the woods to be unnerving at night, but tonight was different. The shadows seemed darker. The full moon less bright. A squirrel scurried by, and she jumped. Sophronia heard leaves crunching behind her. She balled one hand into a fist and turned to see a shadowy figure exiting the woods. Sophronia reared back to throw a punch. Moonlight illuminated the figure as he grabbed her arm.

"It's just me," Edmund said. "I didn't like the idea of you walking in the woods alone this night."

Relief flooded her, but Sophronia smacked Edmund on the arm. "You scared me."

Edmund grinned. "Wanted to help is all."

"Fine. You can carry my sack." She shoved it into his hands.

"What's that?" Edmund pointed to the jade necklace.

"Mama Flora gave it to me. It will serve the same function for me as obsidian will for you."

"You sure you're protected? You can have my stone."

"No, silly, you keep it. Besides, your stone was dedicated to your protection." Sophronia smiled. Edmund was such a worrywart.

The duo followed the path to Hazel's home.

"How are we going to protect the inside of Hazel's home?"

"We're not. Hazel took care of ringing the bell and spreading the herbs while her family worked in the fields this afternoon. She normally cooks the evening meal and said she would have the house to herself." Sophronia peered through the woods. "Here she is."

Hazel joined them at the edge of the clearing. "Where are the stones?"

"Here." Sophronia handed Hazel the stones. "Remember what I told you?"

"Yes."

"Good. Lay the stones and whisper the words. Afterwards, crack open the door for a second, and I'll lay out the salt."

Nodding, Hazel walked off with the crystals in her hands.

Edmund paced, waiting for the signal. Finally, Hazel cracked the door. Quickly, Sophronia and Edmund spread the salt walking clockwise from the northern most point of the house and completing the circle while reciting the words. Tasks completed, Edmund walked Sophronia home and returned to his own. Their nocturnal activities went unnoticed.

The next morning the kids were up early. Chores complete, they were eager to banish Phineas. Now that the others knew what was going to happen, they refused to be left behind.

Jared handed Zacharias, Rebeka, and Hazel their own cleansed and dedicated obsidian tied to a strip of leather that Sophronia had prepared for them. The girls immediately placed the stone around their necks. Zacharias scowled.

"It's for protection from an attacking shade. We all have them," Jared explained. He and Edmund showed their stones to Zacharias and he grudgingly put his on.

"Where's Sophronia's?" Hazel asked, pointing at Sophronia's jade.

She walked past and said, "Old Lady Walker told Jared jade offered the best protection, and Mama Flora recently gave me this. It's been in my family for generations."

As they crossed the bridge to the Hall homestead, Zacharias asked, "Why can we spread the stones and salt the land in daylight at the shade's house? Couldn't we have done all the houses during the day?"

Jared's eyes cut to Sophronia.

Sophronia snorted and picked up the pace. "How would we be able to salt any of our homes, unnoticed, with everyone doing chores outside?"

Zacharias nodded his understanding. "What's the plan?"

This question Jared could answer. He handed Zacharias the cow bell. "You ring the bell. I'll spread the herbs, and Sophronia will place the stones. Edmund will cast the salt circle. We must join hands within the circle in the middle of the ruins. Sophronia and I'll say the chant. Whatever you do, don't break the chain. Once Phineas figures out what we're doing, he will attack. Hopefully, we'll banish him before that happens."

By this time, they had arrived at the ruins of the homestead. Moving quickly, they completed their assignments. Sophronia heard giggling but didn't see Arabella. A few minutes later, the hairs on Sophronia's arms raised, and a chill ran up her spine.

"I'm cold," Hazel said, rubbing her arms.

"Fools. Stop!" Once again, a black mist swirled and became Phineas. He ran at Edmund, but Edmund completed the salt circle in time, and Phineas smacked into an invisible wall. Phineas fell backwards, unable to reach the children. "You don't know what you're doing."

"Yes, we do," Jared said as Edmund joined the circle. The trio recited the final chant.

> "Ashes to ashes. Dust to dust,
> For you we have no trust.
> Blow far away, like a wind gust.
> Be gone from here you must."

The wind howled and Sophronia looked at the form of Phineas still glaring at them. "Again." They repeated the chant, but Phineas was still there, and the wind worsened.

"Let's all say it," Edmund said.

"You must mean it. If you don't truly believe it's the right thing to do, stay silent." Sophronia issued the order, more concerned with banishing Phineas than preventing her friends from finding out the family secret. This time everyone, but Zacharias, said the chant. Small bushes and trees, along with large fallen branches, were sucked into the wind funnel. The salt circle remained connected, unbothered by the wind.

They repeated the chant three times. As the third recitation ended, there was an audible pop and the wind stilled. Debris fell on the teens, and Sophronia grimaced, rubbing a place where a limb hit her shoulder. The salt circle didn't stop the debris from landing on them, but somehow the salt circle wasn't disturbed.

"Is... is it done?" Hazel asked. She pulled twigs and leaves from her hair and smoothed her work apron.

"It is done. I thank you." Arabella stood before them, still translucent but no longer muted.

"Why haven't you moved on?" Jared asked.

"I couldn't leave without thanking you." Arabella's grin widened, and the mist around her turned darker. "Now that Father's gone, his control over me is gone as well, I can have some real fun."

"I knew it." Zacharias left the group and moved toward the edge of the salt circle to face Arabella.

"Zacharias, don't cross the salt," Sophronia yelled.

Checking his boots to make sure he remained safe, Zacharias said, "I knew this was some type of prank."

"I thought you might figure it out, but you're too late. I'm free. Without Father to hold me here, I can go anywhere I wish." Arabella smiled at Sophronia. "And no white witch will be able to stop me. Especially not an untrained one."

Arabella flew circles around the group, unable to cross the salt circle.

Zacharias leaned his head back and spun around, watching her fly. Turning, he grabbed his obsidian, thinking that holding the rock would up its power or something. He tripped on a limb, and the cord broke. He dropped the necklace just as he fell out of the salt circle.

Rebeka screamed.

Arabella cackled in glee and dove for him. She flew Zacharias high as the trees and released him. He crashed to the ground, still outside the salt circle.

His friends forgot all about salt circles and protection spells. They ran to their friend.

Arabella dove at them. Sophronia said, "Form a circle, and repeat the spell."

In concert, the kids recited the words.

> "Ashes to ashes. Dust to dust,
> For you we have no trust.
> Blow far away, like a wind gust.
> Be gone from here you must."

Arabella cackled again. "Foolish little white witch. You dedicated your stones, herbs, and spells to banish Father, not me. Let me show you how it's done."

> "Burn little witch in fire so bright.
> Burn till you are ashes.
> Burn little witch though it's not night.
> Burn just like the branches."

Fire flew from Arabella's fingers straight at Sophronia.

"Stay in a circle. Repeat the chant." Sophronia ran away from the others and, as she suspected, the fire followed her. She turned and touched her jade necklace. Hoping Mama Flora was right, Sophronia watched the fire circle her.

Arabella giggled, until the fire picked up speed. It gathered force, careened away from Sophronia, and turned toward Arabella. "Clever little white witch. You'll pay for this." Arabella flew away with the fire in pursuit.

"You're a witch?" Hazel asked.

Sophronia rejoined the others. "We have to be gone before she returns."

"Look at his leg. We can't move him." Rebeka brushed hair from Zacharias's face. "And he's freezing."

Jared cleared the dirt around his brother. "He landed on half of the old door. It looks sturdy enough. We can carry him that way."

Edmund nodded and moved to the top of the door while Jared moved to the bottom.

Sophronia gathered up the stones around the ruin. They would need to be cleansed and dedicated again.

Edmund and Jared lifted the door with Zacharias on it. They marched quietly down the path. At the bridge, the boys hesitated.

Edmund glanced over at the girls. "You go first. The bridge may not hold our combined weight."

The girls rushed across one by one.

"Go slow. Ease your weight across," Rebeka said.

Edmund stepped on the bridge. It groaned but held.

Hazel pointed at the shade. "Arabella's here!"

*****

Jared glanced behind him and, sure enough, Arabella was almost on him. Edmund was now completely on the bridge. Jared placed one foot on the bridge, and with a crack, a small part of the bridge broke apart. Arabella's scream raised the hairs on the back of his neck, but he was over the water, out of reach. Another crack took more of the bridge.

"Hurry," Sophronia said.

Edmund was across, and Jared had one foot on the ground, when the last vestiges of the bridge gave way. Jared slipped and fell into the creek. Zacharias wobbled, but remained upright, thanks to Sophronia and Rebeka. Each had grabbed a side of the door to keep Zacharias safe.

"See you soon." Arabella's giggle reverberated through the woods long after she faded away.

Hazel asked, "Can she follow us?"

Jared wiped water out of his eyes and stood in three feet of water where the bridge used to be. "Shades can't cross running water, so we should be able to make it home."

"There's no water to the south." Edmund grunted the words as he altered his grip, and Jared took the load back from the girls.

"Yes, that's why our houses are protected. Hurry." Sophronia took the path to her home.

Hugo, Sophronia's younger brother, looked up from the garden and saw them carrying Zacharias. Hugo ran to the house, yelling, "Mama Flora. Someone's hurt."

Mama Flora met them at the door. "Goodness gracious." Clearing her sewing from the table, she said, "Lay him here, door and all."

Subdued, the group didn't speak. Sophronia helped Mama Flora by gathering herbs and items when Mama Flora asked. The others sat in front of the hearth. Hazel stoked the fire so Jared could dry, and she made tea.

"Thank you, child." Mama Flora accepted a cup and took a sip. "Whoever thought to use the door to transport Zacharias, saved him a lot of pain. I've set his leg and both arms. He's lucky he didn't have more broken bones, but it looks like his ribs will be tender for a few days. I also stitched up a couple of cuts, so he'll have scars to remember this by."

Zacharias moaned.

"Easy, child. You're safe. So are your friends." Mama Flora squeezed his shoulder.

Once he was fully awake, the pain registered. Mama Flora gave him a draught, and Zacharias nodded off to sleep. All business, she said, "Jared, you go tell your parents that Zacharias fell. He woke up with no brain issues, but he can't be moved for a few days. Tell your Mama she's welcome anytime. The rest of you head home."

Jared hugged Mama Flora. "Thank you."

"Run along." Mama Flora sent him up the path to his house. Seeing Sophronia's downcast face, Mama Flora said,

"Hugo, finish tending to the garden before your father returns. Josephine, you may help him."

"I don't wanna pick worms," Josephine said.

"Don't matter what we want. Come on." Hugo left with Josephine.

Once the young ones left, Mama Flora turned to Sophronia. "What happened?"

Sophronia hung her head. "You were right. We banished Phineas, and Arabella is free. Zacharias fell out of the salt circle and lost his necklace. She attacked him."

Mama Flora ushered Sophronia to the hearth. "First things first. Come, your father will expect dinner."

After dinner, the medicine wore off, and Zacharias was in great pain. Sophronia joined Mama Flora, and between them, they kept watch. In the early hours of the morning, while Sophronia napped in front of the hearth, Mama Flora felt a presence she had been expecting. She opened the front door. Hovering outside the circle with a murky mist concealing part of her body, was Arabella. She giggled.

"You have no power here," Mama Flora said.

"Shall you stay within the circle forever? Will your son and grandchildren? I am patient and doubt Sophronia can banish me. You failed to train her properly."

Mama Flora shook her head. "I can banish you."

"That's why I'm here." Arabella floated around the edges of the salt circle, but it was sealed properly. "Come out of the circle. Fight me now before the others awaken. Let us end this."

"Agreed." Preparing her attack, Mama Flora walked to the edge of the circle and stepped over the salt, careful not to disturb it. Tossing a dry mixture pulled from her apron pocket, Mama Flora said,

> "Ashes to ashes, I bid you
> Go away you shrew.
> From this earth, I sign your divorce
> From me there's no remorse."

The mist around Arabella grew darker for a moment but cleared. "That weak hex won't banish me." Arabella giggled and dove at Mama Flora. Mama Flora reached for her jade necklace. The one she had given to Sophronia.

*****

Sophronia woke to find the hairs on her arm standing straight up, something she now associated with the arrival of a shade. She checked on Zacharias. He was resting. Noticing the open door, Sophronia looked out in time to see Arabella dive at Mama Flora. Sophronia ran from the house, jumped the salt line, and clutched her jade necklace, silently repeating the phrase Mama Flora had taught her.

Arabella turned and rose back into the air. "You can't protect everyone all the time."

Watching Arabella fade away, Mama Flora said, "She's right."

That same day, Hazel's older brother was injured. His scythe slipped cutting grass for winter fodder to feed the livestock. Mama Flora was able to stitch him up, but he would be laid up for at least a week. Hazel heard Arabella giggle and suspected she had pulled the scythe. Next, Jared stopped his youngest sister from following Arabella to the creek to play. Edmund and Rebeka's younger siblings were tormented by Arabella, who kept appearing to them if they stepped outside the salt circle doing chores. The young ones didn't realize Arabella was a shade for she had a stronger presence now and walked instead of floated to trick the children.

Gathering after their chores were done, Edmund said, "I don't understand. Why is she tormenting, not attacking?"

Jared clenched his teeth. "I think she's playing."

"I think she enjoys fear," Sophronia said. "I have a plan, but it's not going to be easy."

"What do we do?" Jared's eyes narrowed on the woods.

Sophronia explained. Jared's eyes widened, but he said, "I'll distract Arabella. You search."

Sophronia patted Jared's shoulder. "Zacharias can be moved to your house in four days, and the new bridge is nearly complete. We have to banish Arabella after the bridge is rebuilt and before Zacharias goes home."

\*\*\*\*\*

Two days later, amid the long shadows of dusk, Jared watched Sophronia and Edmund cross the newly built bridge over the creek. They headed for the Hall homestead with a three-quarter full moon rising to light their way. He took another path. Once near Arabella's territory, Jared stood in a clearing on his side of the creek, said, "Arabella, can we talk?" He never expected to stand in the woods asking a shade to talk to him, but Sophronia had assured him it would work. Nothing happened. He raised his voice and called, "Arabella."

A dark mist floated to the edge of the water and congealed into Arabella's translucent, hovering form. "Hiding on the other side of the creek? What do you want?"

"Answers. You killed your family and burned the homestead, didn't you?" Jared shivered when Arabella's infuriating giggle was her only response. He threw his shoulders back and said, "Didn't you?"

Arabella nodded. "Family blood makes for more powerful magic. With Father under my control, it was easy. He did my bidding until I killed Mother. He must have truly loved her. His grief broke my hold over him. Before I understood what had happened, he grabbed me from behind and strangled me. Then he buried my body under a pile of rocks. Father was the one who burned the house. I didn't move on, and I discovered he didn't either. His grief and anger somehow gave him the power to contain me."

Stunned by the story she told, Jared said, "There must be some way we can work out an agreement. After all, we set you free."

"Yes, you did. That's why you must die. Can't have you banishing me like you did my father. There is one thing you could do."

"What?"

Arabella smiled. "If the six of you return to me, I'll spare your families."

"We don't trust you."

"I –" Arabella's head swerved around and faced in the direction of her burned out home. "Foolish white witch."

"Wait," Jared said, but she was gone. He hoped Sophronia and Edmund were prepared.

Jared ran through the creek, soaking his feet. He knew where he needed to go. There was a pile of rocks, overgrown with weeds, near the Hall homestead. Hopefully, it was the right location. Jared crashed through the underbrush, tripped a couple of times, and face planted once stumbling over a log. It's hard to run through the woods at night with no path to follow. He ran into the clearing to find Arabella and Sophronia fighting, exchanging spells instead of punches. Arabella was stronger and more experienced, but Sophronia's necklace protected her. Jared grabbed the shovel Sophronia had dropped and ran for the rocks.

Edmund joined Jared, and they moved rocks as fast as they could. Jared reached the dirt and discovered he didn't need the shovel. Phineas had left Arabella's body on top of the ground and simply placed the rocks on her.

Jared pulled out a pouch of salt, sprinkled it on the bones, and used flint to start a spark. Jared said,

> "Burn little witch in fire so bright.
> Burn till you are ashes.
> Burn little witch in this dark night.
> Burn just like the branches."

The spark ignited the bones. Arabella screamed and dove for Jared. It was too late. The fire consumed her bones, Arabella's shape stretched and waved like a flag in the wind. Her scream faded as she did.

Jared gulped in air and asked, "Did it work?"

Sophronia nodded. "I think so. The homestead feels clean."

"Yes, it does, but I'm not sure how I know that." Edmund said. "Let's check on the others."

"What am I going to tell them?" Sophronia's voice was soft.

"Nothing," Jared said. I told Hazel you had found a diary from a great aunt who was a witch. Since Arabella knew your family, she knew your ancestor was a white witch and assumed you were. I explained that between what you found in the diary and what I learned from Old Lady Walker, we worked out what needed to be done. She'll tell the others. Zacharias may have his doubts, but he won't say anything."

The boys dropped in step on either side of Sophronia. As they approached the bridge, Sophronia looked back at the newly scorched earth bathed in moonlight. Her family and friends were safe. Maybe being a white witch wasn't so bad.

As a child, N. R. Tucker wrote short stories about magical places and grand adventures. She never stopped. Her short stories grew into novels. She publishes the occasional poem or memoir, but her first love is the strange or different. N. R. currently publishes two series of novels, short stories, and flash fiction. The *Farseen Chronicles* is an urban fantasy series set primarily in the southeastern United States. The *Finding Earth* series is a science fiction series set on other worlds throughout the stars. Website: nrtucker.com Twitter: @_nrtucker Instagram: _nrtucker Tumblr: nrtucker

## A Land Beyond the Sea

Linda Barnette

## A Land Beyond the Sea

Nothing in this world is as important as family. I learned this lesson many years ago. My name is Bonnie McIver, and this is the story of my family. Even though I'm an old woman now, I remember everything as if it happened yesterday.

When I was a little girl, I lived with my parents and grandparents on the Isle of Skye in our old country, Scotland. My earliest memories are of people gathering around the fire, singing and dancing to the tunes of harmonicas and fiddles. Almost all the men played some sort of musical instrument, and the ladies usually cooked a meat or vegetable stew over the open fire. At some point the music was replaced by talk of politics and other things I didn't understand as a "young 'un," but the men talked often of a land beyond the sea that they called "Amerikay." They had heard of it first from a ship's captain from Skye who had made several crossings and told amazing stories about the sea and the new land. Eventually, the family decided to take their chances and go on a long sea journey to see this new place where life was supposed to be ideal. Even though we were better off than some of our neighbors, things were becoming difficult there because of problems with crops and a lack of work.

So we went to a seaport where big boats brought goods to our country. There were also many other people leaving our homeland. The captains of the ships sold passages on their empty vessels, and all of us boarded our chosen ship. We were able to take only a few of our prized possessions with us. My grandfather took his harmonica; my grandmother took her knitting needles and her Bible; my parents took their wedding quilt; I took my doll, Sally.

We had no idea how difficult the crossing would be: crowded conditions, very scarce food or water, little opportunity to go up on deck for fresh air or exercise, illness, and deprivation.

Some of the passengers were so sick that they did not survive the journey. I think what kept our family going was the music that my grandfather played, the ballads we sang, and the stories we told each other. We also made up songs to sing. My favorite was this one:

"Farewell, farewell, ye cliffs and hills,
the rivers flowing free.
We are going on a journey
to a land beyond the sea.

What we will find and where to live
We leave to God alone.
We are going on a journey
to a land beyond the sea."

Grandfather was a talented musician who played the old songs of our church back in Scotland as well as general music he knew. When I could not sleep, he played quietly to help me drift off. At other times he played for all of the folks who were also worried. He was a wonderful musician and a very kind man.

Most of all, I remember being hungry and thirsty. Some of the sailors cooked great pots of stew, but there was never enough to feed everyone who was on board. Food was scarce, and we often wondered if it had been a mistake in leaving our homeland. Sometimes our stomachs actually hurt from the hunger, and our mouths stayed dry because of the lack of water. We barely had enough to survive, but my family always felt we were doing what God wanted us to do. Luckily, no one in my family ever got so ill that they could not recover.

After three months on the ocean, we finally docked in a place called Philadelphia, Pennsylvania, and found a room in a boarding house. Several of the other passengers also stayed in the same house we did. Both my dad and my grandfather had to find work there so we could save enough money for four horses and a wagon for our trip. My grandfather heard there were mountains like the ones back home in Scotland, so that was where he wanted to go. My grandfather had been a woodworker in our old country and was very lucky to find work as a furniture maker. Because Grandfather missed much of the music from home, he experimented with various kinds of musical instruments trying to figure out something that sounded like his beloved bagpipes. Eventually, he built what was called a "dulcimer," a name that meant "beautiful music." His dulcimer was shaped a lot like a fiddle but had only three strings and was placed on his lap to be played.

Finally, my family saved enough money to buy a Conestoga wagon and a team of four horses to pull the wagon, so we all set out on another long trek down what people called the Great Wagon Road. It began right outside of Philadelphia and seemed endless to me. The road was just a trail the Indians had used for travel called the Warrior Trail. It was not very wide and was often crowded with lots of other wagons.

We slept in the wagon at night, and every evening before bedtime, my mother and grandmother cooked supper in their iron pot over an open fire, just like back home in Scotland. The men caught rabbits and squirrels and sometimes a fish if we were close to a river, and they cleaned and cooked them with various kinds of root vegetables. We had made sure to bring plenty of carrots, potatoes, and turnips from our little garden in Philadelphia with us for our trip as well as a wooden sort of trunk with flour, sugar, and other seasonings. There wasn't a lot of food and certainly almost no variety while we traveled. I thought often of the bread and cakes and scones they used to bake back in Scotland.

Not only did I stay hungry, but the travel was very difficult at times. When it rained, the trail became a sea of mud and was very hard for the horses to pull the wagon. Luckily, ours were not injured at any point down the road; however, one time when it was raining very hard, a horse slipped and caused the other horses and the people on the wagon to fall into the river. The people were able to swim out, but the horses drowned. We felt so sorry for the couple and wondered what they would do. I never did find out if they were able to travel on or not.

I didn't know the names of the places we went through then but have since learned most of them. Crossing rivers such as the Potomac and the Susquehanna was very tricky business. There were sometimes places called fords where the water was low, and that's where we crossed. I thought it was very scary, and the horses didn't like it either! At other places we were able to cross rivers (horses, wagons, and all) on large wooden boats called ferries. Some points of the trail were so narrow that I feared we would all fall into the river like those other horses, but we were lucky. Accidents such as that were fairly common.

A good thing was that there were taverns and a few settlements along the way where folks could stop and spend the night if they wished, purchase food and other supplies, or even find out what the weather was like farther down the road. Otherwise, travel was boring and repetitious except for the music we made and the songs we sang after supper. They were mostly ballads from home. I loved them all because they transported me back to my homeland of mountains and mists, stories, friends, and relatives that we had left behind. Although I liked most all of the songs, my favorites were "Barbara Allen," "Lord Randal," and "The Last Rose of Summer." My favorite tune, other than the one my grandfather made up, was "The Last Rose of Summer." Sometimes I felt as lonely as that last rosebud must have felt.

The loveliest part of our trip was the area through the Shenandoah Valley in a place called "Virginny." The mountains on both sides of the valley reminded us of the mountains in Scotland. Game was plentiful, and there were many beautiful flowering bushes. It was, however, the most dangerous part of the journey because of the high mountains and the narrow roads which were often beside rivers. We were not sure where we would settle, so we decided to keep going. I think that Grandfather felt that he would know when we reached that perfect spot!

Finally, our group made it to a place called North Carolina. Although some of the travelers decided to stop in the flatlands, my family headed for the distant mountains there because we had been told they would remind us of Scotland. We were not sure exactly where we were going, but my grandfather said he would know when he saw it because it would look like home. As we traveled farther, the scenery became spectacularly beautiful. The land was a place of pristine forests, steep mountains, and many waterfalls. It was both beautiful and dangerous, as I remember it. Later I learned that we settled in the area that is now called Blowing Rock, North Carolina.

One evening a group of Cherokees (we had heard about them), rode into our camp. They were yelling and screaming like they were going to kill us all, but the one who was wearing feathers on his head grabbed me and put me up on his horse. Everyone in the camp was very frightened but did not try to shoot the intruders because they did not want to accidentally injure me! I cried and screamed to no avail. The Cherokees carried me off into the night. I was terrified that I might never see my kinfolk again.

The Cherokee village was much different than the village where I was from across the sea and the other ones I had seen in this new world. Their houses were made of clay and twigs and were larger than you would think, with several people living together in one house instead of teepees. However, the chief and his wife, Fawn, lived by themselves, and after I was captured, I lived with them. They had no children, so I was the only child in their house. Obviously, I did not understand their language, but what they called me sounded like Flaming Hair. Years later I would discover that they chose me because of my bright red hair!

I really wanted to go back with my parents and grandparents, but I had no idea where they were or how to get there if I had known. So I decided to do the best I could in my new situation and prayed for God to help me out.

The men were hunters and farmers who raised beans, corn, and squash and also hunted for game. We had quite a variety of meat such as turkey, deer, elk, and small animals like rabbits. Since their village was close to a mountain stream, they caught fish fairly often. Almost everything was cooked over an open fire, which reminded me of how my mother and grandmother cooked our food.

They dressed strangely, I thought, in animal hides and wore shoes called *moccasins*. Their heads were shaved except for a scalp lock, which they wore long. The warriors painted their faces and their bodies, and in the evenings they would play the drums and do strange dances around the fire. The sounds of the drums were nothing like my grandfather's dulcimer. How I longed to hear it again.

Fawn was very pretty with long black hair and a kind face. She showed me many things like different wildflowers and herbs that she used both in her cooking and in making various kinds of medicines. I often went with her to gather them. She was kind and reminded me of my own mum even though mine had hair the color of copper, unlike the long black hair like Fawn had.

Fawn was the healer and treated me as if I were her daughter. She allowed me to be her helper and took me with her when she went to gather the herbs that she used in her medicines. I learned how to identify several herbs and flowers that she used to make medicines that healed the tribe members when they were sick. Fawn also used the fruit from blackberry bushes for a variety of ailments and introduced me to their sweet berries just to eat and enjoy.

The area we were in proved to be perfect for growing many different kinds of plants, all of them new to me. Many of them were also beautiful, like the wild roses. They reminded me of the roses back in Scotland. As time passed, I was happy to learn more medicinal uses of plants: mint for good digestion, boiled sumac leaves for sore throats, and many more. This knowledge later became useful to me as an adult.

One of the best parts of this time was that I became friends with a boy who was about my age, but just a little older. His name was Black Arrow. We played together almost every day. He showed me how to shoot a slingshot and to spear a fish in the water. One day when we were at the river looking for fish, I heard sounds that reminded me of my grandfather playing his dulcimer, but I knew it couldn't be him and stopped thinking about it.

Black Arrow taught me many things about the Cherokee way of life. I loved hearing about the Great Spirit, who was like our God. I had learned about God and Jesus back home but had not realized that other people had different religions. He explained it like this: "The Great Spirit is the chief of all the other gods, such as the spirits of the winds, trees, birds, and other animals." According to Black Arrow, everything had a spirit, and the Great Spirit took care of the Cherokee people. When the older men of the tribe smoked their long pipe, they were connecting with the Great Spirit because they thought all things and all people were connected somehow.

One day when we were looking for herbs for Fawn, Black Arrow's horse stumbled, and my friend fell and hit his head on a rock, that started to bleed profusely. Luckily, I had learned from Fawn how to make a mixture to stop bleeding. I gathered up a bunch of moss and placed it on his head so that it stopped the blood flow. We were both grateful that I could do that. Of course, we told Fawn, and she was thrilled that I had used what I learned from her to save Black Arrow.

Black Arrow told me many stories about the Cherokee, but my favorite one was the legend of the white deer. At an earlier time in their history, there were starvation, hunger, and famine among their tribe. The corn they relied on got some sort of disease and did not produce ears; the beans also died because of the lack of rain. All they had to eat was squash and whatever game or fish that the hunters could catch. Game was scarce because of the drought, and the animals had all moved farther up the mountains in search of food and water. One day the hunting party spotted a few deer grazing in the woods and were preparing their arrows to shoot them. Suddenly another tribe appeared and started to shoot first. Almost immediately, a large snow-white doe stood in front of them and scared the other hunters away. The white deer became a legend among the Cherokee and protected them from time to time when there were great hardships. In his language the white deer was known as *Unega Awi*.

One of the most difficult challenges was learning some of the language. Black Arrow spent hours taking me all around the camp and into the woods, pointing to different things and naming them in his language. I would then repeat his words and name them in my language. It was amazing how quickly I learned enough words to be able to communicate, but then that is far easier for children to do than for adults. I still remember several words, such as *yanosa* for buffalo, animals who used to roam these lands but were forced farther westward by the arrival of both Indians and settlers. I remember the garden words also since I helped to gather food for us to eat. *Selu* was corn, potatoes were *nuna*, squash was called *watsigu*, and bread was *gadu*. It was amazing to me that there were both different kinds of people and also different languages in the world. I had only known others like myself.

Even though the new people were very kind and nice to me, I continued to miss my family and dreamed of seeing them again one day. I missed them so much — their Bible reading and storytelling, cooking, clothing, and most of all, their beautiful music. I cried myself to sleep many nights thinking about them. Sometimes I still thought I could hear my grandfather playing some of our Scottish ballads, but like before, I decided that was not possible and I tried to think of other things. But as time went by, I continued to hear the dulcimer music, and when I told Black Arrow about it, he said that we would try to discover where it was coming from. We packed enough food for one day and set out early the next morning to begin our search. Because the terrain was hilly and rough, we had to be careful not to slip and fall into a stream or a ravine. We walked for a long time, or so it seemed, and saw nothing but woods. We saw no cabin or anything else that indicated civilization. When the sun started to get low in the sky, we headed back to the village.

A few weeks later I heard the music again, and it seemed closer than before. So we left once again to try to find its source. The journey was more difficult this time because I fell from a cliff and hit my head on some rocks, like Black Arrow had done. I was so far down that Black Arrow could not reach me.

I drifted in and out of consciousness and eventually woke up to see a snow-white deer standing over me. She bent down on her knees, allowed me to climb up on her back, and carried me for a few miles with Black Arrow following us. She brought me up to a cabin, and a woman came outside. It was my grandmother! I could hardly believe what was happening was real. She and Black Arrow lifted me from the deer's back and carried me into the cabin, where my surprised parents were doing their daily chores. What a wonderful reunion we had with lots of hugs, kisses, and questions from everyone. My parents assured me that they had searched for me as much as they could but had to travel on with the wagon train. Luckily, my grandmother had become a healer, otherwise known as a Granny woman. She helped the young women during childbirth and also served as doctor in their new settlement. She took care of me and nursed me back to health. I eventually was able to help her learn some of the things I had learned from Fawn.

I loved their little house, which was very different from the houses the Cherokee lived in and was somewhat like our homes in Scotland. It was made of logs that were laid on top of each other, and it also had a little front porch so they could sit outside. Inside there was just one big room with a huge fireplace for heat and a little loft-like place for sleeping. My grandmother and my mother cooked all the food over a big pot in the fireplace, and that reminded me of our trip to these mountains. It seemed like I had been away from the family for a long time, but I had only been with the Cherokee for almost a year.

I asked about my grandfather, who was not in the house with the others. Grandmother told me that he had died from smallpox earlier that year. I told her about hearing the dulcimer, but she told me that that was not possible and that I had just dreamed it up. "You know we don't believe in supernatural events or in spirits, Bonnie. It's against our religion," she scolded gently.

Meanwhile, the family thanked Black Arrow for bringing me home safely even though they were also shocked by his appearance and kind demeanor. Almost everything they had heard about Indians portrayed them as savages. When I started to feel better, my parents, grandmother, and I followed Black Arrow back home, and he introduced them to my Cherokee family. He told his family about the dulcimer music, the fall, the white deer, and about meeting my parents. Both families were very happy about the outcome of the situation, and, strange as it may seem, they all became friends. We even helped them out during the winter when food was scarce. They also helped us when they could.

One evening the next spring we were all together in the cabin when we heard our dog Scottie barking frantically, so we all ran outside. As we looked at Scottie, he was suddenly quiet, his eyes transfixed by the eyes of the dazzling white deer standing before him. Soon the deer vanished into the forest, and we heard a faint melody playing in the background. As the music drifted closer, we realized that it was the hauntingly beautiful sound of grandfather's dulcimer playing the ballad that he had written while traveling down the Great Wagon Road, our much-loved ballad, "The Land Beyond the Sea." Grandmother and the others slowly turned toward me while I closed my eyes and sang the words to the melody that we had grown to love so much.

> "Farewell, farewell, ye cliffs and hills,
> the rivers running free.
> We are going on a journey
> to a land beyond the sea.
>
> What we will find and where to live
> We leave to God above.
> We are going on a journey
> to a land beyond the sea.
>
> Now the journey it has ended
> And home right here we be.
> We love our dear new homeland
> new settlers that we are.
>
> We remember the old homeland,
> the rivers running free,
> But our home in Carolina
> Is that place we chose to be."

From this entire experience I learned several lessons: the importance of family, the fact that family does not have to be related by blood, courage to face the difficulties of life, and faith that things usually work out with the help of God. I continued to love music for the rest of my life and became a writer of stories, poems, and ballads like the ones from both Scotland and our new home. When I look back upon our journey across the ocean, I realize how brave my parents and grandparents were to follow their dreams for a better life. They were willing to risk all that they had for this dream and were among the many early settlers who came together to make America a great nation.

Linda Barnette loves to write about family lore, immersing herself in the in-depth study that goes along with research. She enjoys searching old cemeteries for information on her ancestors and often feels a spiritual connection to those who have passed on. Her favorite writings are closely connected to history and romance. Linda considers the past a wonderful treasure trove of writing topics. She is fascinated by the culture of the southeastern United States and expresses her interest through poetry and short stories. Linda has published many stories and poems about life in the South, including contributing to the Appalachian Memory Keepers and the North Carolina Civil War and Reconstruction History Center.

## Lucius Awakens

Kevin F. Wishon

# Lucius Awakens

Western North Carolina's early settlement has produced many tales, legends, and contentions. Since that time, most of these have been explained, debunked, or resolved. Yet, one story, with its many unresolved questions, remains a curiosity of the region to this day.

It is the story of Lucius Abner Malloy and his wife, Alice Jane Grimes. Indeed, the world's filled with unsavory individuals, and neither Lucius nor Alice will ever occupy the camp of decent folk. Nevertheless, to understand what transpired, we must start by explaining how the New Englander, Lucius Malloy, came to be in western North Carolina.

In his late teens, Lucius began his adventures upon the Atlantic Ocean as a privateer, seizing British goods during the Revolutionary War. In the war's aftermath, Lucius collaborated with two other merchants and made a fortune buying, selling, and shipping goods as far as East Asia. Unexpectedly though, in 1792, Lucius's health failed him, and for months, he was bedridden with an illness. At the same time, Lucius's partners replaced him with another merchant. A resentful Lucius detested the idea of starting over with new partners. So, once he recovered, he took his wealth and retired to the warmer climate of the south.

In 1795, a thirty-seven-year-old Lucius Malloy arrived in Burke County, North Carolina several miles northeast of the Ashlee community. Situated near the Appalachian Mountains, it was quiet there, unlike New England. He chose a section of land bordered by a stream on the north and east sides. Completing the legal requirements of purchase with the local government, he eventually received a document of ownership. Afterward, he built a beautiful home and barn. Also, he planted a large fruit orchard on the property.

A decade later Lucius arrived, the original caretaker of his estate unexpectedly died. To help the caretaker's family, Lucius visited and offered their eldest son the caretaker's job so they would still have an income. Just thirteen-years-old, Hew O'Waine, accepted the position despite his fear of Lucius's temperamental nature.

On the estate, Hew joined two other individuals, Miss Naomi Nettles, the house cook, and young Anna Smith, an orphan, whom Lucius employed as a housemaid. Within a few years, Hew became a competent caretaker of the estate, and Lucius felt relaxed enough to leave the property in his care as he traveled the Carolina coast.

One spring day in 1811, Lucius, now fifty-three years old, decided to marry for the first time. Sadly, though, Lucius treated his bride poorly and spent very little time with her. Eventually, the woman realized the sad truth. Lucius was married to his wealth. The following year, she fell into a state of dark melancholia, and her condition degraded into a severe case of lung fever. Sadly, in the early days of 1813, she passed away. Lucius, with his hard-hearted way, could not even bring himself to attend her burial.

Since his arrival, the locals considered Lucius Abner Malloy an outsider. His wealth and manner towards most people did not help matters either. So, once the news of Lucius's treatment of his bride and her death reached the ears of Ashlee's residents, vicious rumors abounded, painting Lucius as a heartless villain.

Years passed on the Malloy estate without significant change. Lucius was nearly sixty years old. At this point, he began reflecting on his mortality and lack of companionship. In 1817 Lucius once more traveled about the Carolinas looking for someone worthy of his wealth, but his efforts were fruitless.

Now, around this time, a slim woman arrived in the nearby community of Ashlee. She was searching for family members from whom she was separated at birth. With no one in the community remembering the people she sought, the woman, Alice Jane Grimes, began visiting homes outside of Ashlee. Eventually, Alice came to the Malloy estate and met Lucius. Despite her poor background, he fancied her immediately. After a brief courtship, Alice gave up her search, and she married Lucius. Hew, Miss Nettles, and Anna were happy to see Lucius once more take an interest in matters outside of his assets.

Despite his attraction to Alice, Lucius returned to his cold, narcissistic ways after six months of marriage. He was simply a cynical curmudgeon who was unable to keep his attitude positive. Lucius's unkindness came forth in disgusted complaints with no appreciation for any effort Alice made for him. Miss Nettles and Anna grew to dread being in the same room with the two of them. However, Alice was not meek. Soon, she became quite capable of giving Lucius a lecturing he thoroughly despised. While the spring and summer seasons kept the arguments constrained, the cold days of autumn saw these heated discussions gain in frequency.

By the autumn of 1819, Alice had begun taking long walks away from the house, seeking relief from her dismal daily life of dealing with Lucius. One particularly cool fall evening, as the sun began to set, it became apparent to the household that Alice had not returned. Annoyed over the delay of his supper, Lucius directed Hew to retrieve Alice from a trail that bordered a stream where she frequently walked. Quickly, he departed to find her and did not return for some time.

Shrouded in near darkness, the estate had lost all daylight by the time Hew returned. He was shaking, sweating, and breathless. Hew attempted to explain what he had seen. However, Lucius's impatience required him to see it for himself. Carrying an oil lantern, Hew led Lucius to a particularly precarious section of the trail where the path narrowed with a steep drop off to the nearby stream. There, he pointed to deep shoe prints in the soft soil, indicating someone slid off the edge of the bank.

Following Hew's lead, Lucius descended the muddy, leaf-covered bank to reach the water's fringe below. The stream's small bank was lined with dark creek stones jutting up waist high. The rocks, covered in moss near the water's edge, looked like dark ragged teeth in the flickering lantern light. The roar of the fast-moving flow thundered around them, as Lucius looked at the cold waters forcing fearful thoughts from his mind. Joining Hew, he clambered about the cold, damp rocks searching for Alice.

There, several yards away, Lucius saw it. Gleaming along the top of one of the jagged rocks, a reflected beam of lantern light guided them towards a terrible scene. He touched a reflection on the rock, hoping the low light was playing a trick on him. Sadly, it was no trick of the light. The dark, thick fluid was unmistakably partially coagulated blood. Summoning courage, Lucius and Hew pulled themselves up the jagged rocks to look over into the maw of the river. There in the edge of the water, a soaked shawl clung to stones. A portion of the garment tugged at its mooring along the bank as it desperately tried to float away.

Frantically, Lucius and Hew searched both sides of the stream following the water's path for a mile. Sadly, they never found Alice. The flow was deep and swift enough to carry a body away. With many rocky outcroppings and sharp turns in the stream, it was difficult to imagine a body could entirely vanish. Desperate for any possibility, Lucius and Hew expanded their search area to include the woods surrounding the stream. They hoped that Alice had escaped the waters and was lying exhausted and chilled somewhere.

However, after several days, their hopes faded when, after many searches, Alice did not return. Eventually, Lucius concluded Alice had fallen, hit her head, drowned, and was washed away in the stream. Without a body to mourn or bury, Lucius fell into a dark mood for months. Once again, he had lost a companion despite the contentions between them.

Once the news of Alice's missing status reached Ashlee, residents were quick to suspect foul play in the matter. They suggested that as cruel as Lucius had been to his first wife, it wasn't inconceivable Lucius murdered Alice and hid her body. It was a monstrous assertion that only added insult to Lucius's loss.

Following the tragedy, Lucius's disposition remained dismal as he buried himself in the daily management of his property and investments. He took no further interest in romance, preferring instead to review the prosperity of his orchards and livestock.

Two years passed with nothing more about Alice materializing. Despite Lucius's efforts to forget, the tragedy of her passing took its toll on his health. Soon the better part of the week found him in bed listless and upset. Lucius's disposition did not help his situation one bit. A failing heart was later determined to be the cause of his condition. Soon the doctor prescribed medicine along with a healthy dose of advice. Lucius should avoid all stress and focus on leisure for the remainder of his days. It was sound advice, and an average man would have heeded it, but he was far from average.

Despite the doctor's advice, Lucius continued to concern himself with property matters, as much as his health would allow. At least once a week, he would have Hew saddle his horse. Once prepared, Lucius would ride about the property ensuring everything was as it should be. Occasionally, he would make a list of chores he wanted addressed. While Hew worried about Lucius's well-being, this activity did reduce his stress level.

While tragic events on the Malloy estate seemed to have abated, behind the scenes, things were about to get interesting, if not perplexing. By the autumn of 1821, something clandestine was happening in nearby Ashlee.

People do bad things for all sorts of reasons. There are self-preservation, greed, and sadism to list a few. Then, there are those people that do bad things because they have a weakness. They have no desire to do wrong. They simply cannot say no to others enticing them. Such was the case with an idler named Jim. No one knew his last name, but everybody knew his habit. Nevertheless, the community tolerated him. Other than begging the occasional meal, he rarely bothered anyone, which people should have found suspicious, but they did not.

Early one October morning, Jim sat on a tree stump outside the blacksmith's shop on the edge of Ashlee. A chill in the air indicated winter's arrival to Burke County and the nearby Appalachian Mountains. Occasionally, for boarding, Jim would assist the blacksmith by delivering repaired items to the residents. However, that day, he had a visitor. Approaching from behind, the visitor squatted and whispered into Jim's ear.

"Did you bring it?" Jim said aloud.

"Hush. It's time you started working off these favors you owe me."

The visitor pulled a piece of paper from the breast pocket of his dark wool overcoat and stuffed it into Jim's hand. He stared at the paper for a moment and turned to look into the stranger's eyes.

"So, you didn't bring it?"

"Your *medicine* isn't a favor. It has a cost. This task is how you earn it. Once completed, you will have your drink again."

Jim turned to plead with him, but the stranger wasn't interested in hearing it.

"The map and instructions are there. Complete the task as directed, and your *medicine* will arrive as always. Fail to complete this task, Jim, and you will be facing many dry days ahead of you."

Now Jim wasn't aware of it, but he was about to participate in a dirty scheme. However, he was more concerned about his flow of liquid courage drying up, and that alone preempted everything. Still, Jim should have realized after reading the instructions, this task was suspicious. He had learned that the path of least resistance got him the liquid he craved more often than any other. It was a job. It paid in liquor. Jim was going to get it done. Any consequences would be someone else's concern. Gathering his filthy burlap rucksack, he set out walking towards the mountains.

After hours of steady walking, Jim arrived at the edge of a rapidly flowing stream. There, he recognized he had reached a critical location mentioned in the instructions. Rereading the wrinkled piece of paper, Jim memorized the remaining instructions. Wading across the waist deep stream, he set foot on the other side. Thankfully, his body heat and the remaining daylight dried his clothes before the chill of dusk rolled in.

The instructions explained his task: There were nine stone markers in total, each weighing five pounds, that marked the property's boundary. Simply, Jim had to gather all the markers and carry them away.

Lighting an oil lantern, Jim fumbled through the darkness, following the rough drawing in the instructions, which aided him in locating all nine markers. It took him two trips and most of the night, but by dawn, he had them all moved across the stream and stacked in a pile.

Afterward, he slept in a secluded grove of trees for several hours before waking to the intense beams of the afternoon sunlight. Glancing once more at the instructions, Jim noted that there was no mention of how to dispose of the markers. Remembering something he had seen nearby, Jim laid the stones in his burlap rucksack and pulled them until he reached a pasture.

Pleased with his efforts, Jim returned to Ashlee and waited for Jackson, his mysterious visitor, to bring his reward. His eyes began to tear up as he thought about the delicious stupor he would enjoy over the next few days. Alternatively, once his actions were discovered, tears of frustration and despair were bound to flow.

Three days later, Lucius undertook his weekly property inspection by horseback. Despite his ill health, very little escaped his notice, and on that day in October, Lucius immediately noticed something missing. Angry and full of suspicion, Lucius rapidly rode back home. Soon, he found the caretaker, Hew, in the orchard.

Hew helped a winded Lucius down from the saddle and assisted him to the porch where he collapsed into one of the evening chairs. After drinking a glass of water, Lucius finally relaxed enough to relate what he had discovered. After several clarifications, Hew understood a few stone property markers were missing.

Perplexed, Hew asked, "Who would do such a thing?"

"I'm not certain. I suspect it's an attempt to create uncertainty with the boundary lines and steal property from me."

Hew marveled at Lucius's ability to deduce a motive behind the occurrence. Immediately, Lucius instructed him to survey the whole property to ensure that all other markers were still in place. However, Hew's search discovered, not a few, but all the property markers were missing.

The matter seemed inexplicable and did nothing to improve Lucius's health. His anger over the issue drove him to determine who had done this. Days afterward, Lucius instructed Hew to travel about the Burke County area, asking residents for information regarding the matter. Eventually, only the Ashlee community remained unquestioned when news of Lucius's mental breakdown reached Hew. Left with no other choice, Hew returned to Lucius's bedside.

There in bed, Lucius remained for months, as he struggled to recover from the despondency that had taken hold of him. Hew wanted to resume the search but, instead, stayed by Lucius's side. Daily, Hew tried to cheer him with good news about the progress of cattle or crops on his estate. Despite his effort, Lucius sank deeper into despair as paranoia consumed him.

The removal of the stone markers had taken a toll. Hew, Miss Nettles, and Anna, all tried to comfort him, declaring it was the work of an adolescent prankster. Alas, their efforts were all for naught. In the days that followed, Lucius Malloy's health declined further. His weak heart could no longer bear the stress. One cold day, in January 1823, as Miss Nettles descended the stairs to prepare the morning meal, she found Lucius dead on the mid-floor landing. Apparently, he had risen in the night attempting to leave his room. However, Lucius only had enough stamina to make it a short distance before his heart gave out. There he sat down on the stairway landing and departed this world.

Alice's death had been terrible, but Lucius's death cast a dark pall over them all. Hew barely remembered digging the grave out by the edge of the old apple orchard. It had been Lucius's favorite place on the property. In this sad loss, it was small comfort for Hew, Miss Nettles, and Anna to bury him there.

Uncertain of what to do, the three continued working on the property fulfilling their obligations. Once the news of Lucius's death reached the Ashlee community, George Lauten, Lucius's associate and lawyer, visited the Malloy estate. After being welcomed by the household, George was quick to tell them Lucius had left a will. Eager to learn it's contents, they encouraged George Lauten to dispense with formality and read the will. To their shocked amazement, George asked for one of the three to retrieve the will.

"Are you not in possession of the will?" Hew asked.

Briefly, George explained that Lucius had not made the will available to him, preferring instead, to keep it secured within his private study. After a thorough search, the legal document remained undiscovered. Undaunted, George encouraged them to continue the search, assuring them he would return for a reading of the will. However, the following day, a message was hand-delivered to the

Malloy estate requesting the three to come to visit George Lauten in his office the next morning.

Anna, Miss Nettles, and Hew left the Malloy estate before dawn by horseback. They reached the community of Ashlee by nine that same morning. After having the local blacksmith replace a horseshoe Hew's mare had thrown while crossing some rough terrain, they made their way to George Lauten's office and walked into the shock of their lives. For there, standing next to the attorney, was the very Alice Jane Grimes herself.

The shock on their faces was unmistakable, and Hew fell back against the door as though he had seen a spirit. George Lauten rushed over and seized him with both hands insisting he would explain everything. Disturbed by the appearance, Miss Nettles and Anna stared at Alice for several moments as Hew sat, drinking a glass of water. After George felt everyone had recovered, he assured them, they were neither hallucinating, nor deceived. Now, Alice Grimes had remained quiet up until this moment, but then she spoke.

"How are you, Hew, Miss Nettles, and dear Anna?"

Hew couldn't answer her. Instead, he asked the crucial question screaming to come out of him.

"How…?"

"How am I alive? You mean to ask?" Alice said, completing his question.

Alice smiled and turned her head to one side.

"I — I don't know. I can't remember."

Troubled and confused, Hew looked to George for an answer. In his formal way, he explained that Alice had been waiting for him in his office when he returned from the Malloy estate. Miss Nettles looked at him with skepticism, but he assured her that this was truly Alice Jane Grimes. George had confirmed it by a necklace she was wearing, which Lucius Malloy had given Alice on their wedding day. George Lauten was one of the few guests in attendance the day they were married.

Agitated, Hew insisted he had seen the deep shoe prints in the soil and the shawl in the water, which meant this couldn't be Alice. George turned to Alice and asked her to share the story she had told him the previous day.

"Early on, I tried to recall things, but I couldn't. When the fog in my mind receded, I was in the care of an elderly couple who said they had found me lying by a stream. Apparently, at some point, I hit my head. Then, after several months, what started as brief mental flashes slowly gave way to the realization of who I was."

"But the blood...," Hew insisted.

"Yes, I sustained a terrible injury to the side of my head. You can't see the scar because my hair covers it. Be assured it was quite severe. My kind caretakers told me so. Thankfully, the injury was not permanent, and now, I've returned home."

At this point, George Lauten intervened and continued the story. The previous day, he had revealed the news of Lucius's death to Alice. However, she had heard about his death earlier and seemed unshaken by the news. Realizing her connection to Lucius Malloy, Alice came to George Lauten's office to make her return known. Alice admitted she feared no one would believe her, but if she did not return soon, she knew she would lose her home.

Then George Lauten carefully explained that unless Hew O'Waine, Miss Nettles, or Anna could produce a will stating otherwise, the Malloy home and property belonged to Alice because she was the surviving spouse of Lucius Malloy.

Neither of the three could produce a will.

"Very well, then! It has been some time since I've slept in a place I can call my own," Alice said. "Let's return home."

The three prepared to depart. Then, Alice paused to make a remark.

"All except for you, Hew. I no longer require your services. Please remove your personal belongings from the caretaker's cottage. Another caretaker will be residing there soon."

Hew was stunned. He could not recall if he said anything or even nodded after Alice spoke.

Moments later, George Lauten and Hew stood in the parlor looking out the window. Hew was sipping brandy from a small glass George had offered him to help ease the impact of the day's ordeals. To pour salt on the wound, Hew watched as Miss Nettles and Anna rode by, heading out of Ashlee, accompanied by Alice riding the mare Hew had ridden into town. As a light shower began to mist down, Hew couldn't help but feel a little vengeful.

"I hope you're soaked by the time you get home!"

George Lauten patted Hew on the shoulder and said, "Come on, Hew. Don't be that way. I know you don't mean it. You can start over now, here in Ashlee. I'll try to put a good word…"

A stare from Hew caused the sentence to freeze in George's throat.

"Oh well, nevertheless, I'll do what I can to help you," he said sheepishly. George had forgotten that most of the residents of Ashlee had a low opinion of Lucius Malloy, and they would transfer that condemnation on to Hew.

"Where will you go tonight?" George asked.

"I reckon I'll walk back to the caretaker's cottage and sleep there tonight. Probably, collect my belongings in the morning, and return to Ashlee by tomorrow evening," Hew said.

"Come and see me when you return to Ashlee. Hopefully, I will have some employment for you by then."

Hew set the empty brandy glass on the side table and shook George's hand.

"Thank you. I appreciate anything you can do."

Hew opened the door departing into the damp and cloudy afternoon. Pulling his coat collar up against his neck to shut out the cold, Hew set out walking toward the Malloy caretaker's cottage. He knew darkness would arrive soon, so he walked quickly to reach his destination.

The following day Hew returned to Ashlee in the afternoon and briefly met with George Lauten. Giving Hew the list, George apologized for the lack of opportunities on the paper, but Hew assured him it was fine and he was grateful.

"If Lucius were here, he would expect me to do all I could to help you, so when those opportunities run out, come and see me."

Hew did not reply. Instead, he nodded and shook George Lauten's hand. Lucius Malloy, and anyone associated with him, was undesirable in Ashlee, so he would not be bothering George for any future favors.

Walking towards the home of the first opportunity on the list, Hew considered the timing of his situation. He was thankful that his mother had passed on, and his siblings no longer lived with him in the caretaker's cottage. It would have made this situation far more challenging.

Two weeks passed before Hew's temporary work dried up. Then he found himself walking through Ashlee after dusk with nowhere to sleep. Trying to find relief from the bitter cold, the warmth of the blacksmith shop forge drew him. At least there, Hew could feel a little heat from the furnace near the doorway. Shortly, the blacksmith caught sight of Hew and called to him.

"Aye there! Do I owe you any blacksmithing work?"

Hew was embarrassed to respond. Previously, he had come there riding on a fine mare. Now, he was wearing a burlap cloak made from feed sacks to ward off exposure from the winter's chill.

"No. You owe me nothing. I'm just here for the warmth."

"Well, come in and tell me your story. It's a slow evening, and I could do with a break." The burly man motioned Hew to come in.

Hew entered the blacksmith's shop and admitted who he was and his situation. It was cathartic to tell someone the whole story and have them listen. After finishing, they both sat silently watching the light from the furnace flickering and dancing against the shop walls.

"Aye. That is a tragic story, indeed. I heard Old Man Malloy had passed away. I also heard there had been some drama before his death. However, I'm usually too busy to indulge in regular gossip."

Pausing, the blacksmith scratched his head and thought.

"Do you realize I may be the only resident in Ashlee who truly knows your story? The rest of the town just speculates based on rumors they've heard."

Hew nodded and said, "Lucius Malloy was difficult to deal with, but he was good to my family and me. Unfortunately, others do not share my feelings, so I should move on before I hurt your reputation with my presence."

"Nonsense! I'll not hear of it. Nobody tells me what to do. They don't want to upset me. I'm too important," the blacksmith said with a wink.

"You can stay here anytime you like. There are clean stalls in the back with straw. Bed down back there and rest. Never you mind the other fellow back there. He's a local sot sleeping off a recent souse. Don't worry, though. He won't bother you."

Hew gathered his sack of belongings and found an unoccupied stall in the back of the blacksmith's shop. There he bedded down in the straw and rested for a bit. Soon, Hew fell asleep. Just as he began to snore, a voice from somewhere nearby interrupted his doze. Hew ignored the voice speaking incomprehensibly. Hours later, the sound of a hammer plinking against an anvil pulled him from his slumber. It was still early, and the sun had not risen, but the birds were excitedly chirping in anticipation of an early spring.

Hew struggled to find work over the next week and often shared blacksmith delivery errands with Jim, the idle drunkard. Jim had been the other fellow talking in his sleep, Hew's first night in the blacksmith's shop. He felt guilty taking what little work there was from Jim, but the drunk didn't seem to mind. He was happy to have company.

*****

Now back on the Malloy estate, it was the month of March. Alice had settled into the Malloy home decorating it to brighten things up. Finally, she had gotten what she wanted. However, she still had a few loose ends that needed addressing. Jackson, her co-conspirator, who had orchestrated her death, disappearance, and other mayhem, was an issue that needed to vanish. Then, there was the undiscovered legal will problem. Lastly, it had been two months since she fired Hew. With spring rapidly approaching, Alice needed to employ a new caretaker.

News of her acquiring the Malloy estate had spread about Ashlee by March. The community suspicioned it was the work of conniving, so, they switched their belief that Lucius had murdered Alice. They now believed Alice had orchestrated the whole matter and returned just in time to claim Lucius's legacy. Thus, the locals called Alice *Dirty Jane* thereafter.

*****

However, Ashlee's change of mind about the matter didn't help Hew. The locals still hadn't lost their distaste for Lucius and continued to cast their disdain on Hew by refusing to help him. Thankfully, the blacksmith did not share the town's opinion, which enabled Hew to have a place to sleep at night. Additionally, he had someone to talk to when Jim wasn't shaking off the effects of a drinking binge.

Jim shared all the unpleasant gossip that flowed around Ashlee with Hew, including rumors, which demeaned Lucius Malloy. Hew didn't try defending Lucius's character. Instead, he listened. Strangely, Jim never discovered Hew's background. On the other hand, Hew never disclosed his origin to Jim. It was one less embarrassment he had to endure. Therefore, his backstory remained unrevealed until early one morning when Jim, once again, woke Hew talking in his sleep.

When Hew stepped into the stall where Jim was sleeping, he called out Jim's name. Unaffected, Jim continued having his deep dream conversation. Annoyed, Hew was tempted to shake Jim awake until he heard a portion of Jim's conversation.

"No- no. Please, just bring me more drink. I'll do another chore for you if you want me to…"

"I did a good job on the last chore. I followed your instructions and did everything. I even made those cornerstones vanish. They'll never find them!"

Hew was thankful he was patient with Jim. By chance, he had discovered the very person who had removed the property markers. It had been months since Lucius directed Hew to locate the stolen markers. Although Hew had failed to find the stones while Lucius was alive, he still felt inclined to complete the request. Finally, this revelation gave him the chance to complete Lucius's request. Reaching down, he grabbed Jim by the shoulders and shook him hard until the drunk's bleary eyes fell open and he cried out in shock.

"Don't hurt me! I don't have any money."

"It's me, Hew! You were talking in your sleep."

"Oh, is that all? Leave me alone, and let me sleep."

"Trust me, Jim. I'd like to, but you have one last chore to complete!"

"Huh? What?"

Jim had just rolled over in the hay when Hew dropped the last comment on him. Rolling back over, he asked Hew what he meant. At this point, Hew regained his assertiveness. He now felt he was acting on Lucius Malloy's behalf.

"You stole those property marker stones, and now, you are going to return them."

"Ho — how do you know that?" Jim asked, suspiciously.

Hew was tempted to laugh. Instead, he sternly explained to Jim that he had admitted to it while talking in his sleep. Very few people in Ashlee knew all of the markers had vanished. Hew explained that only the person who stole the markers would know this fact. Hew was bluffing, but it was all he needed to say to get Jim's confession.

"So what if I did? What does it matter to you? It shouldn't bother a fellow like you. You're just like me. You don't own a thing in this world!"

Jim's words stung his pride a bit, so it made what Hew had to say next easy.

"You don't know who I once was. I was a property caretaker for an estate northwest of here owned by Lucius Malloy. Does that sound familiar?"

Jim blinked several times and looked hard at Hew.

"So, why are you here? You have a good job!"

"I had a good job, you mean! Lucius Malloy's health declined after you removed those property markers, and he died. Then I got the sack from the new property owner," Hew said.

"I didn't know anything about that. I just did a task for someone, and that is all I know. None of this is my problem."

"I think a judge would disagree. If you don't help me locate those property markers and put them back, I'm going to tell everyone what you did. You think it's hard to get your drink now.

I'm willing to bet it's near impossible to get a drink when you are locked up!"

This comment got Jim's attention. He cared little about most things, but anything that would separate him from liquor was something he could not ignore. He did not like what Hew was asking him to do, but if Hew followed through with his threat, Jim would be forced to flee town.

"If I help you return those stones, will you help me get a drink?" Jim asked.

"I'm pretty sure I don't owe you anything. But, if you mend the mess you've made, we will see."

Hew coerced a grumpy Jim to get up and take him to where he had hidden the stones. In the early morning hours, the two set out northward towards large tracts of farmland. After some time, they came to a field bordered by a stone-wall fence, and Jim stopped and sat down against the newly laid wall.

"We don't have time to rest. You need to help me locate those markers!" Hew exclaimed.

"We are here," Jim said, nodding towards the wall. "Somewhere in there, are the nine stones you seek."

Hew almost collapsed when he looked at the wall made up of dozens of fieldstones that stretched out for some distance. After looking at the wall, Hew noticed something that saved the day. The stone property markers were a different color from the majority of fieldstones that made up the wall.

Hew was thoroughly upset with Jim. So, he showed it by making Jim retrieve the marker stones stacked within the wall as Hew found them. It was late in the afternoon by the time the two men recovered the last stone markers. Jim was slow and eventually required Hew's help to remove the last two stones. Once gathered, the two dragged the nine stones to the stream that bordered the Malloy property. There Hew and Jim left them hidden until the following night.

Jim didn't talk in his sleep that evening. He was too exhausted. Instead, he slept soundly and late into the morning. After running a few errands for the blacksmith, the two took early naps that evening and woke just before midnight. Crawling out of the hay, they lit a lantern and disappeared into the moonlit night.

Arriving at the stream bordering the Malloy estate, Hew assisted Jim in transferring the nine stone markers across the waters. With Hew's help, moving the markers across took a shorter amount of time than it had taken Jim initially. Thankfully, the one good thing Jim did was to keep the map and directions Jackson had given him. Hew shuttled the closest stones to their proper location on the property but left Jim to restore the most distant markers using the map and lantern.

It still took most of the night to return the stones. Jim struggled to find the proper location for the last marker. With Hew's assistance, they eventually located the divot left from its original placement. As they placed the last stone in its proper place, Hew and Jim breathed a sigh of relief. Then they returned to Ashlee before dawn with the satisfaction of a fulfilled responsibility and restored integrity.

By now, the deceptive treachery that Alice had orchestrated was glaringly obvious. However, that morning, just before dawn, something troubling arrived with the desire to right a wrong. Maybe a hole was torn in the fabric of the universe, or the power of anger and revenge coalesced. Either way, had anyone been present in the apple orchard of the Malloy estate on that morning, they would have been speechless, for the specter of Lucius Malloy awakened.

Over several months, Hew discovered much by questioning Jim about the stranger named Jackson, who had befriended Jim over a year earlier by supplying his habit generously. That was until Jim completed the errand for Jackson and received a meager amount of drink for his efforts. Jim had pleaded with him for another chore to earn more liquor, but apparently, Jackson had what he wanted, so he left Jim high and dry.

Hew had time on his hands, so he used it to analyze the details of the treachery that had cost him his caretaker's position. Soon, Hew determined that Alice and Jackson were in cahoots. Although Jackson's long-term motivations were not clear, Alice's were apparent to even the residents of Ashlee. Lucius's wealth was the flame that had attracted all the parasites.

Now in truth, as his wife, Alice would have received Lucius's property upon his passing. However, Hew surmised that Lucius Malloy wasn't dying fast enough for Alice and Jackson, so they, at some point, conspired to fast forward Lucius's life with tragedy and conspiracy. Hew wasn't sure if Alice had been conspiring with Jackson from the start, but he was confident that her original alibi for being in Ashlee was merely a ruse. She had no missing family. Alice was interested in meeting Lucius and getting into his wealth.

With each passing day of the summer of 1823, Hew felt his assumptions were correct and was tempted to approach George Lauten with his thoughts. Whether he was right or not, it still did not change one crucial factor. Hew was penniless, and any effort to maneuver Dirty Jane from her undeserved throne would be costly.

Therefore, by autumn, Hew was thoroughly discouraged over the matter. Depressed, he dreamed about escaping to another area with better work prospects. With winter already returning to the Appalachian Mountains, Hew dreaded the thought of sleeping in the near-freezing temperatures of the hay stall for another year. Thankfully, foul weather delayed his departure. For that same week, George Lauten visited Hew by horseback and told him something interesting had transpired.

"Whatever it is, I'm no longer interested. I'm moving on with my life, and I don't have time for digging up old bones or gossiping!"

"But, wait. You haven't heard the news."

"Sorry, George. I'm not interested."

Frustrated by Hew's dismissal, George leaned over in the saddle of his horse and handed Hew a folded letter.

"If you won't listen to me, then maybe you'll listen to someone else. Either way, come see me when you have shaken off your despair and opened your ears to reason."

Hew reached out and took the letter from his hand. Without another word, George clicked his tongue and directed the horse on its way. Hew felt ashamed of how coldly he had treated him. His attitude had soured over the summer when he realized what happened right before his eyes.

George Lauten and his horse disappeared from view in the steady September drizzle. In the street, hoof prints left by George's horse were already filling with water as Hew stepped back under the shelter of the blacksmith's shop and opened the multi-folded letter.

September 21, 1823

Mr. George Lauten:

Sir, I require your assistance regarding matters of the Lucius Abner Malloy estate. I am aware that you addressed this matter several months ago. However, I now hold documentation that legally states otherwise. Please locate the previous caretaker, Hew O'Waine, and have him visit the Malloy estate forthwith. I would very much appreciate it. Please inform him that he has no reason to be concerned about Alice Malloy. A week ago, she fled the Malloy home, disturbed and paranoid. I do not expect Alice ever to return. Nevertheless, it does not matter. Alice's name is not in the will.

Sincerely,<br>Miss Naomi Nettles

Hew wasted no time in returning on foot to the Malloy estate. When he arrived, all of his clothes were soaked.

"Come in. Oh, I'm so glad George Lauten found you!" Miss Nettles gushed.

Hew was soon seated by the fireplace and dressed in fresh clothes. After a brief meal, Miss Nettles, joined by Anna, sat with Hew and showed him the document they had found. There it was, clearly written in Lucius's handwriting, the will they had all searched for thoroughly.

"Where did you find it?" Hew asked.

Miss Nettles and Anna looked at each other.

"Well, come on. Where did you find it?"

Miss Nettles explained that after Alice fled the house. Anna began cleaning the bedroom and found the will on the mantle of the fireplace. As far as they could tell, Alice had possession of the will, but for how long, no one knew.

"And look who the will's benefactor is!" Anna said.

Miss Nettles unrolled the will ultimately revealing Hew O'Waine as the beneficiary of the Malloy property in full. Also, the executor listed was George Lauten. However, one detail shocked all three of them. The date handwritten at the top of the will was February 28, 1819.

"I… I don't understand. Why would Lucius bequeath me all of this while he was still married to Alice? She didn't die- I mean disappear until the autumn of 1819," Hew said.

"Well here's another question for you," Miss Nettles added. "Why would Alice ever leave this will to be found? Would she not have destroyed the document in the fireplace as soon as she found it? She had control of everything."

The three sat for hours in front of the fire, discussing the matter and the peculiar way things had worked out. Shortly after midnight, Anna departed for bed, leaving Hew and Miss Nettles alone to talk.

"I have something else I want to show you. I didn't show Anna this because I'm not sure what to make of it."

Miss Nettles reached deep into the pocket of her apron and produced a small worn book. Its corners were bent over from wear, and its spine wrinkled from usage. She handed it to Hew and continued.

"It's Alice's diary. I found it outside, lying in the entranceway of the house not far from the porch. I've read a little, but I wanted you to read it. I hope it will explain some of her bizarre behavior."

Hew took the book from her hand and flipped through the pages looking for entries dated around the time Alice arrived on the Malloy estate. Most of those entries appeared innocuous, and if there was anything surreptitious going on, she had not written about it. Later entries though, began to show the true nature of Dirty Jane.

Looking at the 1819 entries, Hew could see they were short and full of hate for Lucius. In one entry, Hew read where Alice first met Jackson in March of the year she disappeared. Her entries continued even after her feigned death in the autumn of 1819, proving she was conscious of all her actions. Apparently, Alice and

Jackson had absconded to Virginia. There they hid until Lucius Malloy's death.

Hew skipped entries from the winter and early spring of 1823. He knew those events painfully well and did not want to read about it. In April of that year, Hew found an entry where Jackson had visited the Malloy estate and had a conversation with Alice. After several sentences, Hew discovered Alice's link to Jackson. They were lovers, or at least that's what Jackson thought. In one entry, Alice called him a "weak-hearted criminal" and mocked him, writing she never planned to share the wealth with a fool such as him. She cold-heartedly led him along using him.

"Do you remember a man coming to see Alice this past spring? I've heard he wears a dark wool jacket and goes by the name Jackson."

Miss Nettles thought for a moment, and then her face lit up when she realized of whom Hew was speaking.

"That sounds like the man who came to see Alice last spring. They met privately and talked for hours. I thought he was here to replace you as the caretaker. Later I suspicioned that there was something strange about that visit. When he left, he was furious about something, but Alice did not appear to be upset in the least."

"I'm not surprised. This fellow thought Alice was going to share the inheritance with him. She used him to pull off her scheme and then dumped him. Alice eventually paid him to go away," he said.

Miss Nettles leaned back wide-eyed with her mouth hanging open.

"The audacity!"

"Oh, by the way, I found the man who took the property markers. Jackson paid a local drunkard to remove and hide the stones. Alice and Jackson did it to push Lucius over the edge," Hew added.

Hew and Miss Nettles sat silently, sentimentally remembering Lucius and his eccentric ways. After a few moments, Hew raised the diary and thumbed over a couple of pages.

"Who is this caretaker she replaced me with?"

122

A strange look crossed Miss Nettles face. Alternating shades of light and darkness from the flickering wood fire highlighted a dubious look on her face.

"She hired someone? When and who was it? I asked her once if she were ever going to hire someone to replace you. She said she had hired someone, but I never saw anybody."

"Really? Are you sure? She mentions hiring a caretaker by the name of Alaster. You never met him?"

"No," Miss Nettles said emphatically. "When I had an opportunity, I would trim vegetation away from the house, but the livestock had to be cared for, so most of the pruning was left undone. No one has been here maintaining this place since you left."

Hew flipped through several more pages of the diary perusing the entries for the name of the replacement caretaker.

"Strange, she mentions this Alaster fellow in quite a few entries over the summer."

"That woman was off her rocker! No one's been here, but Anna, Alice, and me for the last eight months. What in creation was wrong with her?"

Hew wasn't listening to Miss Nettles anymore. His face was stricken as he continued reading. When Miss Nettles asked him what was wrong, he held up his hand, desiring her to wait. After reading several of Alice's summer entries, Hew lowered the diary and stared at Miss Nettles.

"Well, I did tell you that peculiar things occurred. So, I'm guessing that's what you just read. Am I right?"

"Peculiar doesn't start to explain what I've just read. Was Alice sleeping at night? 'Cause she wrote several entries in here where she walked around at night and saw strange things."

"After May, she began to mumble to herself and do strange things. She ordered the fancy drapes you see over the windows, and in June, started complaining that moths were destroying them. I looked for them, and so did Anna. There were no moths. It was all in her head."

Hew listened to Miss Nettles for a moment and thought about Alice's behavior. She had been so brazen, patient, and callous in her efforts to acquire the Malloy property. It was difficult to imagine anything rattling her.

"Miss Nettles, do you-."

"Please call me, Naomi."

"Naomi, do you think guilt from this plotting and scheming caused Alice to lose her mind?"

"It's possible, but I don't know. Madness usually progresses over time. This happened abruptly, and I saw no prior indication of it. Still, Alice was carrying a load of stress keeping all those lids on steaming pots and making sure nothing boiled over!"

"True. But, something was tormenting Alice."

Hew turned a page and read another entry. After a moment, he looked up at Naomi.

"This entry mentions a night she was locked in her bedroom. All those bedroom doors lock from the inside. How could she have been locked in?"

"Well, she wasn't," Naomi replied. "I found her sleepwalking or having a phantasm. Her bedroom was in shambles. Everything had been torn off the walls. Her fingernails were broken, shredded, and bleeding. I asked her what was going on, and she said I had locked her in there. As she described being locked up, I realized she was talking about being in the cellar, not her bedroom."

"Well, did she tell you about her nightmare when reptiles, foliage, and briars invaded her bedroom?" Hew asked.

"What?"

Naomi moved to Hew's side and read the entry for herself. Alice had scrawled the entry in shaky handwritten letters, but the words clearly described the very thing Hew had stated.

"My word! That woman was seriously disturbed."

"Yes, maybe, but look at this." Hew pointed to a previous entry. In it, Alice described a conversation with Alaster.

"Alice was angry about the appearance of the estate. She cussed Alaster and told him she was not pleased with his work as a caretaker. Isn't it odd the following night she has a nightmare about it?" Hew noted.

"You are telling me! Look at this. She described waking up to vines, briars, and branches covering her bedspread. When she sat up in bed, she saw that the whole room was being encroached on by vegetation. Then lizards, snakes, moths, and rats emerged from the greenery, covered the floor, and converged on Alice sitting in bed. She pulled the bedspread up to keep them from getting to her," Naomi said.

Pointing to another entry, Hew said, "Look at this. Alice described waking up and getting dressed. When she looked in the mirror, the image reflected was terrifying. As she brushed her hair, it began to come out, and her teeth as well. She had become an old hag!"

Excited, Hew pointed to another sentence in the diary.

"Whoa, here's the entry where she described finding the will! Lucius hid it in the walls of his study. Alice wrote that she saw a vision of Lucius hiding the will. So, she went to the study, found the specific piece of trim molding, and removed it, revealing a secret compartment containing the missing will."

Hew stopped for a moment while Naomi read the entry he had summarized. Hew continued and found more evidence proving his suspicions

"Well, well! Would you look at that? Alice knew Lucius changed the will in 1819, and she was very upset about it. Apparently, Lucius realized what kind of person Alice was and took steps to prevent her from getting control of his wealth. He hid the will to prevent her from finding it."

"Finally, an explanation as to why Lucius changed the will and made you benefactor," Naomi noted.

Flipping through the remainder of the diary, Hew noticed that there were few entries left. So, he skimmed the pages getting an idea of what happened to Alice in her final days on the Malloy estate. Closing the diary, Hew leaned back in the chair and looked at Naomi.

"It got worse. It seems Alice could no longer determine reality from a dream."

"I can believe it. Alice hardly spoke to Anna or me in the last three weeks before she vanished."

Hew nodded and continued.

"She was excited to have the will in her possession. And she tried to destroy it in the fireplace just as you speculated. However, the will reappeared on the mantle the next day unscorched. She even tore it up once, but, it appeared whole on the mantle the following day. Frustrated, she poured lantern oil over the will and lit it on fire on her bedroom floor."

"That's where that charred spot on her bedroom floor came from!" Naomi exclaimed.

"Well, let's be glad she failed! Her last entry revealed how delirious she was. She said when she tried to burn the will with lantern oil, she caught the whole house on fire and burned it down. Alice described finding Anna and yourself dead after the fire. The reason she fled was she thought that everything and everyone in the house was lost."

Looking over at the very much alive Naomi, he added, "Clearly she'd lost her mind."

Naomi looked at him, dubiously. "Really? How exactly did she find the will we all searched for unsuccessfully? Then explain to me why the will was never destroyed, and lastly, who was Alaster?"

Hew shrugged his shoulders and stood to go to bed. "Simply put, some things in this world defy explanation."

Days later, Hew visited George Lauten and apologized for his behavior. George forgave Hew, and with the will, helped him finalize his ownership of the Malloy estate.

Afterward, Hew returned and took over the estate, putting everything back in order, as it had once been when Lucius owned the property. Hew could have chosen someone better, but he installed idle Jim as his new caretaker. The way Hew saw it, if not for Jim's help, he would have never known the truth.

Several months passed, and after much flirting, Hew asked Naomi Nettles to be his wife. They were married a few days later. On his wedding night, Hew stood, looking out the bedroom window across the apple orchard. There, in the moonlight, he could have sworn he saw Lucius Malloy looking up at him. Hew started to call to him, but the figure turned and walked towards the old orchard. Hew had doubted for a time, but now, he began to wonder.

If Kevin F. Wishon isn't fixing something broke at home, he is probably figuring out how to break and redeem the protagonist in many of the adventure stories he writes. Drawing on various career and life experiences, he blends it all together with a heavy dose of imagination to write entertaining, educating, and encouraging compositions. Kevin's stories of trials, trauma, and disaster make for intriguing adventure fiction, which is his primary writing genre. However, he also writes short stories and poetry, which occasionally appear in the Davie County Enterprise-Record newspaper. Currently editing several works of fiction, Kevin looks forward to publishing his personal work in 2020.

Lucius Awakens

# The Legend of Little Happy Foot

Stephanie Williams Dean

The stifling humidity of summer hung like a thick blanket of smoke, robbing the boy of oxygen. He struggled to breathe, inhaling in rapid, shallow gasps. His brown eyes reflected the royal blue sky filled with billowing, black storm clouds. In between the dark masses, a blazing sun scorched the dry, dusty ground on which he lay.

The boy's mind wandered from sun to rain. The ground of the plain was barren, dead from lack of rain. There had been no moisture in weeks — not a single drop of water. Creeks had almost dried up, and the river on which their village had been built was the lowest he remembered. Today looked promising as the sky was clustered with varying shades of light and dark gray and fast-moving clouds.

A few days before, his people had prepared for hunt with their usual rituals of constant prayer, fasting, and a purification with black drink. They sang songs about the animals they hunted. He thought of the rain dance he'd performed at the village ceremony the evening before as his people waited patiently for a sign. Continuous fields of corn were threatened to be lost.

But more than rain, the boy needed protection from the sun's burning rays. The great light had extinguished for three days during which time he waited for someone to come. There was a cave close by if only he could drag himself into it. He tried to lift both legs to stand up, but they were dead weight. He attempted to roll over, but his body wouldn't turn in either direction. Becoming delirious and barely able to whisper, he spoke to the spirits of the animals he'd hunted. The young boy began to feel faint and dizzy. His vision was now a blur of color.

He attempted to sing magical songs that would drive off sickness and conjure good spirits — with special words that were responsible for keeping away malevolent spirits and preserving good health. With all the strength he could muster, the boy whispered and chanted incantations required to make peace. His people followed these rituals because creatures, like man, had been given the power to breathe. He evoked the spirit of the deer with special words in his mind.

> Here a deer lies on the ground,
> you're not dead, but awake to join.
>
> Here a deer rests quietly in grass,
> and sleeps until he joins another.
>
> Here a deer awakes to the spirit,
> now like one, he joins the others.
>
> Here a deer, his spirit now gone,
> and joined another, and lives right on.

At an early age, his parents had dedicated the boy to the study of medicine. Now his hand reached for the leather pouch attached to his skirt, and his fingers untied the strings. He grasped the polished quartz charm inside, one he'd taken from his amulet collection before leaving his village. He carried one with him at all times because malevolent spirits played a role in causing sickness.

He'd never seen one but had heard about the three-foot little people and was afraid of them as they exacted misfortune on his people. Knowing he would one day be a medicine man, he spoke special chants while using his secret charms to keep them away. Knowledge of these matters had been handed down to him from many generations.

The flies buzzed around him, landing on his burnt skin and sucking the blood from it. With stone in hand, the boy turned his face toward the sun. He was a child of the sun, and the great light was his source of life. He remembered once being scolded for shooting his arrows overhead towards the sky. Thinking of his dead father, the boy vowed to get revenge by inflicting crying blood for his death. He would seek revenge, and his heart would be fully satisfied. He dreamed of the attack, planning to travel at night, hide in the woods, and then attack at daybreak. He was good at covering his tracks and rearranging the leaves and earth on which he might step so there'd be no telltale signs left behind. Many years earlier, his people had been among the first to confront the flood of settlers who intruded on his homelands.

He wasn't sure what was happening now. There were constant, piercing pains in his stomach and back. He began to see visions of his village's giant mound, and his thoughts drifted back to the dead once again. One after another, the dead were covered with enormous piles of dirt. The boy dreamed of his village's sacred fire — one that always burned in the temple. The mounds were shaped like cones and surrounded his village dwellings, and their dwellings were surrounded by cornfields — now withered and dried up from lack of rain. He remembered the days he helped tend and plant their fields.

The boy believed he must be dreaming. Maybe his thoughts were only experiences of his spirit while asleep. His spirit moved at will during the night, but it was now daylight. For such a hot day, he felt chilled, and his teeth chattered against one another. He wished he could feel the protective warmth of an animal skin against his own. The boy longed to be back in his village where he loved to fish. He dreamed of deer, bear, and buffalo skins that felt good against his skin. The image of the sacred albino deer came to mind.

He considered whether he was dying. Death was to be feared and sorrowed. The boy was afraid to die. And besides that, he didn't want his family to suffer cry-times — a time of retreat, fasting, and covering of their heads while mourning death. Surely he was drifting off to sleep.

And then the long-awaited rain came. The blue sky turned the blackest black, and there was no longer a sliver of light. All the boy's pain was gone. He ascended in graceful circles, drawing closer to the magnificent, azure sky. The great vast of blue was now completely clear without a single cloud. Looking down, he saw nothing but traces of dead grasses, now saturated, the remains of dried up bushes and withered trees — and a small framed, brown-washed, smooth-skinned and hairless body of a young boy. With a full head of straight black hair, and far too young to have it shaved, the boy recognized himself — the lively fire dancer known as Little Happy Foot.

*****

At daybreak, Little Happy Foot's father and two uncles had descended from the plateau on horseback to sell some of the village's pottery to the plains settlers. The trade works from their village were extensive and highly sought after. Art was important to them, especially pottery works made for funeral purposes. The significance of their artistic techniques had increased over time as sacred animals such as the hawk, crow, wolf, and cougar were often pictured. Each piece of pottery was unique and artistic — and was stamped or imprinted before firing by pressing wooden objects into the clay.

The boy had learned much about forming and decorating pottery from both his mother and father. His people collected mica, fossil shark teeth, and granite crystals used for artistic decoration from the nearby mountainous area. Every boy in his village was required to learn how to make a bow and arrows, a primary weapon and hunting tool. Of all the young warriors, Little Happy Foot was one of the most skilled boys at making weapons. He looked forward to turning seventeen when he would be ceremoniously inducted into the group of hunter-warriors — even if it were only a symbolic honor.

Later, rogue settlers had viciously assailed Little Happy Foot's people without provocation. The outlaws had planned a surprise attack at daybreak. As the men from his village drove their stallions down from the mountain plateau to the foothill plains, they were ambushed by surprise, caught in a line of gunfire, and killed. The outlaws robbed the men of their horses, weapons, leathers, and tack along with the valuable crafts made by his people. The boy watched as the scoundrels loaded the pottery into large, leather bags attached to the sides of their saddles. Hidden behind bushes and thickets of thorn, the bad men did not see the boy as he was out of sight. But he saw them clearly.

The dead bodies lay on the sun-scorched ground for two days until folk from the village came in search for them. They didn't

133

discover the boy who had followed the group of men. He was a short distance away, partially hidden by brush. In a hurry, the Indians didn't want to linger long at the site for fear the outlaws might still be nearby. It wasn't uncommon for Little Happy Foot's people to be punished by rogue settlers who sought vengeance on those who had chosen to remain on the land that had always belonged to the Indians. For the most part, Little Happy Foot and his people lived relatively close to the settlers' village and peacefully.

Unbeknownst to the others, the boy had followed a short distance behind the men. He wanted more than anything to be a great warrior like his father. He had begun to prepare for the age when he would be able to go hunt for days with the older men. But the boy was somewhere between being an older boy and younger warrior and was not allowed to accompany them. Many days, he would follow behind without their knowledge just to watch them from a distance.

In the past, his people were an organized and mighty nation. As time went on, numerous small groups separated from the whole, and small villages sprang up in different places. Happy Foot's village was now a small group of no more than 200 whose community was on a river. Here they lived quietly and traded peacefully with the settlers who lived down on the plains forest. They sold handmade canoes crafted from hollow tree trunks, drum, and calumets, sticks for ball play, axes, war clubs, dressed deer, and buffalo hides. Little Happy Foot and his two younger brothers contributed to the work that had to be done by his family.

*****

Delighted with her new shoes, Lila tried on the pair of skin moccasins. Papa had given them to her as a gift, and she'd loved the shoes from the day she received them. They were ruggedly worn, which surprised her as Papa was a very gifted shoemaker. He was especially good at sewing and repairing their family's shoes. She wondered where Papa had gotten the pair of small moccasins and to whom they had belonged.

Lila loved to dance, and when wearing the shoes, she felt almost magical — like her feet never touched the floor as she moved across the room. The shoes made her feel powerful and so grown up. She loved the way they felt on her feet with the soft hide next to her skin. She ran her fingertips across the satin leather. They were made by hand with unique beads made from rocks. Lila's older sister, Agatha, secretly wished she had a pair.

Ever since Lila learned to dance so gracefully and beautifully, Agatha's boyfriend, Zack, paid less attention to the older sister — and his eyes were always on Lila. Of course, Lila never noticed and didn't pay the older boy any mind as she was only thirteen-years-old and had no interest in boys. Agatha was in love with Zack and relentless in doing anything she could to recapture his attention.

Several weeks earlier, the girls' father, Levi Walton, had ridden his horse up to an area where the plains met the mountains to hunt small game. He also planned to meet with some Indians to trade his vegetable crops for a few of their artistically designed leather goods.

The Waltons' town existed partially in forested country – in the great Eastern woodlands where live oaks, stately pine trees, and tall cypresses stood. But, summers were hard as the ground was barren and dry. The family had much difficulty clearing land, planting food, and keeping it watered for plants and vegetables to grow, so food had been scarce. Levi saved every drop of water in barrels.

While out hunting, Levi made a gruesome discovery when he came upon the cadaverous, pale body of a young boy, still dressed in his animal skins with a penetrating gunshot wound that had ripped through his back and exited out his stomach. The grim scene made it obvious the boy had lost ghastly amounts of blood. Levi was not sure what had happened.

The Indians of the plateau and settlers of the plains had lived peacefully for many years. They often traded commodities and helped one another by selling or trading their wares and produce. But sometimes they heard tales of disquieting, rogue outlaws who would lay in wait at the foot of the plateau for the men to come down to the lower plains on horseback seeking to sell their wares. The outlaws ambushed, terrified, and killed, stealing horses, tack, bows and arrows, and anything else of value. Levi feared what dreadful thing might have happened. The young father was repulsed by such a mean and hideous crime as the boy was still a child. Even those hair-raising outlaws weren't known to kill children.

In the unnerving days long past, the killing of innocent women and children was always considered revolting. These crimes were deemed to be abominable and cowardly by even the most loathsome of men.

Levi gently picked up the boy's corpse and carried it to a small, dark cave nearby. There, the boy's grisly body would be concealed until he could return to bury him.

Before leaving the site of the heinous crime, Levi glanced at the boy's handmade moccasins and then quickly untied and slipped them off his feet. Having no intention of disrespect, the father thought the shoes would make a nice souvenir for his daughter, Lila. The boy looked to be around the same age and size of his youngest daughter. Taking after her father, Lila had always admired the Indians's handmade, high-quality craft made from animal skins. She begged her father to trade for a pair. But the men would not sell their shoes to the settlers, saying they were used in dance ceremonies that held special significance in their village.

Levi knew his daughter would be excited when she saw the shoes. He was sure it made no difference to bury the boy without moccasins. The most important thing would be to bury him because, according to the beliefs of the Indians, if not buried, his spirit would wander forever. The mountain main's beliefs focused on their duties to the dead. They believed in the immortality of the soul. When one left this world, the soul was to go live in another world to be rewarded or punished. Levi knew the customs of these men. Burial was very important to their belief system, and they had great concern for the role of spirit. They were not to be buried with their head to the west as that's from where bad spirits came. They believed there were differences between body and spirit. If not buried, one's ghostlike spirit would be forever haunting the grounds. Although not superstitious, Levi respected the boy's customs and vowed he'd come back soon and do what was necessary.

Weeks later, Lila's mother, Flora, and Levi were outside working in the garden when their daughters returned from the schoolhouse. The family dog, Mick, greeted Lila and Agatha as they approached the house. Lila reached down to pet Mick's furry head. Wagging his tail, the dog followed her into the four-room house for his daily treat. She knelt on her knees and let Mick lick her face. He barked at her.

"Oh, you're such a fierce beast, aren't you," laughed Lila. "OK. Here's your treat." She held a biscuit in the air, and the dog quietly waited.

"Good boy, Mick. You're such a good doggie." She gave Mick the treat after he had followed her command to sit.

Lila was proud because she had trained the dog herself, and he was obedient. She wiped his drool off her skin.

The first thing Lila usually did was her chores after returning home from school — that is until she'd received those moccasins. She changed into her play clothes and donned the soft, worn shoes. After sliding them on, she began to dance wildly. What an uncanny ability to dance she possessed now. She'd never danced like that before she got the shoes.

There was a knock on the front door. Zack had stopped by the house to see Agatha — or so Agatha thought. When the older sister opened the door, Zack sauntered in, making a beeline to Lila.

"Wait a minute, Zack. I want you to taste something I baked," Agatha said, trying to get Zack's attention away from Lila.

"Just a minute, Agatha. Wow, I didn't know Lila could dance this good. I want to watch — she's such a beautiful dancer." He appeared mesmerized, and his eyes remained focused on the younger of the two sisters.

"Oh, hi, Zack." Lila focused on her dancing and ignored the boy.

"Can you show me how to dance like that?" Zack asked. "Where'd you learn that anyway? It's kind of a cross between a foot stomp and a pow-wow."

While Lila was dancing away, Mick began to growl ferociously. The dog sprang to all fours with wiry hairs bristling along his back. He barked at one wall, but weirdly, there was nothing there. Snarling, with lips peeled away from his teeth, the dog exposed his sharp teeth. He then crouched down and inched forward, indicating an imminent attack.

Lila immediately stopped dancing as she knew something was terribly wrong.

"Mick, come," she commanded. The dog ignored her command and continued to inch toward the wall with his beastly teeth bared.

All of a sudden, a picture hanging on the wall mysteriously moved and now hung eerily crooked, which unnerved everyone in the room. In the hair-raising moment, the dog sprang forward, bizarrely alternating between a whimper and a bark, and could not be calmed.

"Gee, that was weird, did you see that?" Zack directed his question at Agatha. "That picture just moved."

"I guess you think our house is haunted," Agatha replied sarcastically, rolling her eyes. "I saw no such ghostly thing. I'm surprised you saw anything but Lila," the older sister ribbed the boy but didn't acknowledge the unexpected event that had just taken place.

"No, really. I'm not kidding. That creepy picture just went from hanging straight to crooked. That creeped me out!"

"Well, I guess Lila has made the ground move for you." Agatha taunted. "Make your dog shut up, Lila."

Lila wrapped her arms around Mick trying to soothe the dog, but he continued to bark.

"I told you that stupid dog was poorly trained," Agatha huffed, hoping Zack would notice the poor job Lila had done teaching her dog.

Zack walked over closer to the picture and stared at the frightful, family photo. Suddenly, he jumped back and let out a spine-chilling scream.

"Gee whiz, her eyes just moved from side to side," Zack exclaimed in a shocked voice. He shuddered when he felt something touch his shoulder. He whirled around, but no one was there.

Alarmed, Lila stopped dancing and tiptoed over to the dark portrait of her grandmother. "I didn't see anything move," she said calmly. Lila noticed that the spooky picture now hung crooked on the wall.

"I guess I just imagined it, after all," Zack said, his voice still quivering.

Agatha moved closer, hesitating, yet still managing to take another jab at her sister, and said, "Lila, you'd do anything for attention, wouldn't you?"

"Don't blame me. I wasn't even close to the picture," Lila retorted.

Confident she could win Zack's attention back, Agatha pointed out, "You know how thirteen-year-old girls are; they're always trying to get the attention of older boys."

"I wish you could dance like her," Zack replied, looking wistfully at Lila.

"Well, I can do lots of things better than Lila – like cooking, for instance. She's not as good a cook as I am," Agatha retorted, feeling both insecure from Zack's lack of interest and discouraged by her lack of confidence.

Lila felt herself getting angry but kept quiet for a minute, trying to think of a come-back to her sister's self-serving comment. Yeah, Agatha could cook better than she could, but hey, her older sister was starting to get a little bit chubby.

"Well, by the look of your thigh that resembles a ham hock hanging in Papa's barn, you'd be better off cooking and eating less, and working a lot more."

No sooner had the words left her mouth, than Lila felt bad. She was never one to be mean. Her sister brought out the worst in her. Agatha was furious, and Zack, feeling uncomfortable, tried his best to change the subject. And for a moment, everyone forgot about the portrait.

Letting out a loud sigh, Lila sat down and slid off her shoes. She was exhausted. She'd never danced like that or for so long. Lila thought about how strange it was that she could dance so beautifully when she'd never been that good before. The young girl had begun to believe that the shoes possessed a magical power that allowed her to dance for hours.

"Those moccasins are like magic," she shared with her family at the dinner table.

Levi corrected her quickly, saying, "There's no such thing as magic, Lila. You've just found something you're really good at."

Jealous of how complimentary her father was toward her sister, Agatha spoke up.

"Well, you'd think she planned to earn her way dancing. She rarely gets her chores done on time. And when she's supposed to be doing her homework in the afternoon, she's entertaining boys. I think she's gone boy crazy."

"You're just jealous because your boyfriend likes me better than he likes you," Lila accidentally blurted out, now having trouble restraining herself.

Not wanting Lila to have control of the situation, Agatha clarified Zack's intentions, "No man wants a little girl. And certainly not a tomboy. Zack likes girls, not tomboys. He enjoys more refined girls," she said, batting her eyelashes at her sister.

"La-di-dah," Lila said. She wasn't going to let her sister suck her into being mean again. She didn't care for boys anyway. They were too much trouble and always saying dumb stuff. Lila knew she was a smart girl and enjoyed learning new skills. She hadn't met a boy yet who knew as much as she did about taking care of things on the land. And she was skilled — she could do most of the things boys could do, only better.

Agatha was a girly girl. How boring, Lila thought. Her sister could cook and clean house so she might make a good wife, but Agatha would hardly be as useful as Lila to a man. Lila grew plants and flowers and harvested food for cooking. She cared for livestock, helped deliver babies, and fed the babies when their mothers died.

Because Lila had a keen interest in nature, she learned much more than her older sister who stayed inside the house most of the time. There was much to be learned from a man. Lila couldn't wait until she turned fourteen so her dad would teach her how to shoot a rifle. Then when she turned fifteen, he would teach her how to handle a pistol. Maybe he would take her with him to hunt small game.

While Lila silently ate her dinner at the table, she observed her father and sister in conversation. Agatha had Levi's handsome features. With long dark hair and dark eyes, she had a very mysterious look about her. With skin like porcelain and beautiful white teeth, she was the object of every young man's desire. Lila, on the other hand, with her blond braids and blue eyes, looked more like her mother.

Then came the sound of a deep, guttural growl. Mick, who was lying on the floor, raised his head and bared his teeth. Again, the dog sprang to his feet and barked nonstop at Lila's father. Mick began to run around the room with his ears straight back and all hairs on his back bristling while continuing to bark.

"You need to get rid of that dog. He's starting to become a nuisance and is quite annoying," Agatha said disgustedly. "Thank goodness, my cat is quiet."

An empty chair ominously moved away from the table turning all heads in the room. Lila looked at her father. He stared at the chair at the table. Lila's mother's mouth dropped, and she jumped up and moved away from the chair, which was next to her.

"Lila, did you do that?" Levi asked with a look of bewilderment on his face.

Now concerned due to her father's expression, Lila answered, "No, I didn't do anything."

Agatha looked irritated. "You did it, didn't you? Lila's trying to scare us again like she did the other day when Zack was here. She moved that old picture on the wall so we'd think there was a ghost in the house."

Getting more upset, Lila couldn't contain her feelings any longer, yelling at her sister, "You probably pushed the chair with your foot just so that you could blame me for it."

The family heard a loud thud as if something had fallen in the next room. Lila got up from the table and walked in the room to investigate. From the corner of her eye, Lila thought she saw an illusory shape move across the room and then frightfully disappear. The candle on the table began to flicker, and the fire went out. Cold chills ran over Lila's body, and she felt a mist of something cool and wet touch her face. Lila felt the presence of something in that room.

In the darkness, she barely made out the outline of a wraithlike figure in the corner of the room.

As Lila quickly returned to the kitchen, the chair moved again, pushing back toward the table. This time, everyone at the table stood up and backed away. Lila looked at her father, who had an alarmed look on his face. Oh, this is spooky, Lila thought. She had the distinct feeling someone was strangely watching them, but there was no one else in the room, not even an old ghost.

"Ok, girls, there's nothing to be frightened of," said Levi, who came around to the side of the table to inspect the chair, pulling it out and then pushing it back in.

"I'm sure there's a perfectly reasonable explanation for everything. Seems there's nothing wrong with this chair," her father said while turning it upside down to inspect it further.

Levi tried to convince his family as much as he tried to convince himself. He felt an ominous chill as if someone had walked past him. Petrified, Levi didn't say a word, not wanting to scare his family further. Only the standing hairs on his neck revealed his grim fear.

Before Levi could get back to his seat and sit down, the same chair flew up in the air and crashed down on the other side of the room. In another unnerving moment, the father's metal dinner plate went flying upward like a disc and spinning back down on the table, scattering food all over.

By this time, Agatha's terrified cat sprang to her feet and with arched back and all hairs standing on end, stood stiff as a board, hissing at something no one could see.

Lila's mother let out a horrifying scream and ran from the room. Levi desperately tried to go after the chair and grab his plate simultaneously. Now he knew this was no coincidence. Agatha ran from the house and followed Flora outside while Lila sat calmly in her chair.

"Well, it does appear we have a ghost living here," she softly suggested, trying not to alarm her father. But down deep, she was distraught. Oh, no, a ghost. She had heard of other folks' homes being haunted by spirits of dead people, but she had no experience with spectral beings. She felt the uncanny presence of something standing behind her. The room had turned so chillingly cold that Lila could see her breath in front of her face when she spoke.

"Hogwash. That's not divine, and there's no such thing as ghosts." Her dad responded.

"Well, I don't think it's the great Holy Ghost, so it must be a spookish spirit of another kind. What else would send chairs flying across the room?"

After things calmed down that night, Lila lay in the small bed next to her sister in the bedroom they shared. "Lila. Lila. Are you asleep? Are you going to tell me that you really believe in ghosts?" Agatha asked in a mocking voice.

Lila anticipated another put down from her sister, so she pretended to be asleep. Of course, she believed in ghosts. There was such a thing as spirits of dead people. What a dumb question. That was the problem with her sister. She might be pretty, but she wasn't smart.

The next day after the two sisters returned from school, Lila pulled the moccasins over her feet. The young girl rubbed her fingers across the soft fur that lined the tops. The tips of her index finger and thumb stroked the exquisite, shiny, blue, and red beads. Each bead was delicately cut from stone and colored with ink.

Like before, no sooner had she put the shoes on her feet than she felt the urge to dance wildly.

"I've gotten sick and tired of your dancing. That's all you ever do now, and you've neglected your work," Agatha noted, hoping to discourage Lila from dancing before Zack arrived. He came every day now to watch the young girl.

"You're just upset because you can't dance," Lila answered, tired of her sister's constant jabs. Lila was getting better at standing up for herself.

Believing that her sister was chasing her boyfriend, Agatha reminded Lila, "Zack is not interested in you. He loves me. We're going to get married one day. So, you can dance all you want, but you won't win him over. Zack only has eyes for me."

"Well, maybe if you were a bit smarter, but you've got a ways to go," Lila snapped back at Agatha.

Not able to contain the mean words boiling up inside her, Lila continued, saying, "Men like women who can do more than boil soup and then eat it. Besides, you better learn to dance — have you seen your backside lately?"

Agatha could take no more and began to cry. Lila was disgusted, thinking her sister didn't like the taste of her own medicine. Then came a knock on the front door. Agatha wiped her eyes and answered it. Zack was carrying some fresh eggs his mother had sent over for Flora.

"Oh, Zack, you're so thoughtful. I didn't know you were coming to see me today. Excuse me, I just cut up onions, and my eyes are watering." Agatha lied, not wanting Zack to know she'd been crying. Lila let out an exasperated sigh.

Zack barely acknowledged the older sister and walked right past her toward the kitchen to put down the eggs. But he was sidetracked by Lila's dancing.

"I want to watch Lila for a while. Hey, Lila, how about giving me some lessons. Your dancing reminds me of the Indians's ghost dancing."

"Oh, Zack…I just baked some cookies, would you like one with tea?" Agatha asked in her sweetest voice, although now more furious at Lila than ever.

"Yeah, maybe in a minute," he answered disinterestedly.

Zack still had the eggs in his hands and had forgotten to go to the kitchen. He slowly sat down, mesmerized by Lila's rhythmic dancing. He was drawn to the girl with her long, blond braids and innocent blue eyes. Her suntanned skin and dirty face betrayed her true nature. She was a tough, outdoorsy girl and was not the kind to stay inside for long. Zack loved that about her. He had already grown bored with Lila's older sister, and his eyes were now only on the younger of the two. He envisioned one day when she might be his wife.

While daydreaming of his and Lila's future together, Zack's basket of eggs flew out of his hands and up over his head. Every single egg broke, and slimy yellow yolks dripped off his brown hair onto his clean, white shirt.

Lila stopped dancing, "Oh my, Zack. My goodness. What happened?"

"I don't know. I'm not sure. I didn't do anything."

"Now, Zack. Don't worry. I'll help you get this mess she made cleaned up," said Agatha, rushing over to the boy's side. "What did you do, Lila, knock the basket over with your arms while doing your crazy dancing? You're the clumsiest girl." Agatha imitated the younger sister, wildly waving her arms around in the air.

"She didn't do anything," Zack said, taking up for Lila. "I must have accidentally dropped them," he reluctantly admitted.

"On your head? Nonsense. Of course, she did. How else did you get eggs on your head? I'm sure Lila caused every bit of this," Agatha accused.

Then, the dreadful sound of an offensive whisper came from the corner of the room as an apparitional shadow moved across the wall. Only one word was recognizable, "Lila. Lila."

The three kids stood paralyzed, unable to move for a few seconds. For the rest of the night, the two sisters and Zack busied themselves, managing to stay distracted from what they'd seen and heard. Levi prohibited the children to speak one more word about any of it.

*****

The heat of late summer was upon them, and everyone was cranky because of the extreme temperature. Lila's mom and dad came in from working in the gardens and were sweaty. There was just no way to stay cool. Lila made sure she didn't put her moccasins on until evening when the day cooled down a bit. Otherwise, she'd be sweating like crazy. Zack changed his routine, coming later to see the young sister dance. Frightful happenings continued to occur, but Levi assured his family of no worries, telling them there was a reasonable explanation for all of it. He encouraged his girls to read their Bibles more often. Wanting to believe their father, the family resumed daily activities, putting the paranormal circumstances out of their minds.

Agatha stayed mad at Lila. It was very apparent now that Zack had no interest whatsoever in the older girl and made that obvious to everyone. Agatha had taken her anger out on her sister and, in Lila's opinion, was making a fool of herself trying to win back the boy's attention.

"If you would leave him alone, he might like you again. You're the one who's always chasing after him," Lila told Agatha, giving it right back to her sister.

Agatha couldn't accept the fact that her boyfriend was now in love with her little sister, who was nowhere near as beautiful as she was. Zack still came over to their house every night after dinner. He'd bring one gift or another for the family as his excuse for coming, but Agatha knew he was really coming to see Lila. Lila tried to advise her older sister, but Agatha wouldn't listen to the younger girl, believing she was too out of touch with boys to have any good advice. But, Lila had many boyfriends in their town. She understood how boys thought. While some boys liked a woman who could maintain a good house, boys loved girls who helped them, as her Mamma helped her Papa.

One night at dinner, Lila, once again, quietly suggested to her family that she believed they had a ghost in their house. Agatha howled in laughter over Lila's belief, and no one else in the family took her seriously.

"All right. Believe what you want. Just wait and see," she told them. "Not only do we have a ghost, but I believe the ghost is trying to tell us something, and the activity is starting to get more intense," she warned them.

"And, I've been paying close attention to when the ghost presents itself. It most assuredly does not like Zack or you, Agatha."

"That's ridiculous. Why not me?" asked Agatha, trying not to buy into the younger sister's theory. "Why would any ghost not like me?" She immediately felt foolish for coming off like she might believe her younger sister's nonsense.

"You will have to figure that out for yourself, but it seems the ghost's attention does not set favorably on either of you."

That night, when Lila put on her dancing moccasins, she knew the ghost would appear again. It sometimes seemed like her dancing called forth the spirit. When Zack arrived as he usually did in the early evening, Lila's feet were already prancing gracefully across the floor. Agatha had given up trying to get Zack's attention and now concentrated her efforts on pointing out Lila's shortcomings, hoping the boy would notice and lose interest in the girl.

"Every time you wear those shoes and dance, something bad happens. I'm weary of cleaning up the mess you make," Agatha said.

No sooner had Agatha spoken, when a picture on the wall came smashing to the floor right beside her. Scared to death, Agatha ran from the room. Zack kneeled to pick up the picture when a heavy, iron lantern fell off the fireplace mantle, barely missing the boy's head. Standing up, Zack said, "I'm out of here, too. This is getting scary, Lila. I'm worried about you staying in this house by yourself. Let's go get your dad."

Zack grabbed Lila's arm and tried to pull her with him, but when she wouldn't go, he gave up and stayed in the house to defend her.

"I'm not afraid. The spirit is my friend and protector. Show yourself, old Ghost," she cried out to the invisible presence. "Show yourself to me in the name of the great dancing spirit."

Lila had tied a few things together in her mind. It was no coincidence that almost every time she wore the moccasins, she danced, and the spirit appeared. The spirit liked her and seemed to protect her from her sister's harsh words and shield her from the attention of Zack.

"Come forth, I say." Lila cried out to the spirit as Zack watched on in horror as the ghastly, wavy shape of a dead, young, mountain boy appeared.

"What do you want from me?" Lila asked, trying to sound brave. "What do you come to my home for, and why do you come when I dance in the moccasins?"

Lila winced, looking at the corpse standing in front of her. The apparition was a boy with hollow eyes and sloughing, knotty skin. The ghost held his deformed arms out to her as if to indicate he wanted something from her.

Right then, the laces of Lila's moccasins spontaneously untied, and the beads begin to flutter as if the air was beneath them.

Sitting down, she said, "Yes, I knew it all along — it's these moccasins, isn't it? What do you want with these shoes, ghost boy?"

Suddenly, the shoes flew off her feet and were now laying on the floor in front of her. When Lila finally understood, only then did the ghost disappear.

Later that night while at dinner, Lila brought up the strange visit from the ghost. She was no longer afraid of him.

"Lila, I've told you, our family doesn't believe in ghosts," said Levi. "There's no such thing. I'm forbid any further mention of ghosts in this house."

"Papa, then tell me where those moccasins came from. Where did you get them? Tell me the story of how you traded for the shoes."

"Oh, stop being dramatic, Lila," said Agatha. "You really have a problem — so needy for attention, trying to make everyone believe our house is haunted. Is there anything you wouldn't stop at to get Zack's attention?"

Ignoring the bickering girl, Levi went on to explain, saying, "One morning, I was out hunting near the plateau when I came across the body of a young mountain boy – and he was dead. I'm not sure what had happened there. Maybe he was involved in a battle with some outlaws passing through the area.

"Are you saying you took them off a dead Indian boy's feet?" asked Lila in an incredulous voice. "Don't you know how important it is to bury his belongings with him? What happened to the boy?" Lila asked with widened eyes, now afraid to hear any more.

"Well, I took his shoes off because I knew how much you had admired their moccasins. I carried his body to a nearby cave and planned to go back and bury him, but I never found time to go back."

"You mean his body is still laying in the cave and has not been buried?" Lila asked alarmedly. She knew immediately what was wrong.

Indians believed that if a body was not buried, the soul would wander the earth forever. Lila had to make sure her father went back and properly buried the boy. Otherwise, she and her family would never rest in peace either.

148

"I knew it. I just knew it," said Lila. "There had to be some explanation for why those shoes made me dance and why the spirit came to this house. Those shoes are calling forth the boy's spirit. He's appearing to me now — in spirit. His spirit is wandering these lands and will forever more until he's buried."

"But still, a spirit being here in this house sounds a bit far-fetched to me, Lila." her dad said, not wanting to believe the girl.

"Well, you know Lila, she thinks she knows everything. She knows better than everyone, and she chooses what she wants to believe," Agatha said in a disapproving tone of voice, trying to gain her father's approval.

After Agatha spoke, several pieces of pottery slid right off the kitchen table and crashed down on the floor, breaking into pieces. Her dad stared at the dishes, horrified.

Shooting a nasty glance in the direction of her older sister, Lila commented, "Oh, really? What do you believe now? You're truly dumber than I thought you were. You just don't get it, do you?"

Agatha and Flora ran from the room again. Lila knew she and her dad would have to take care of this situation as her mom and older sister were going to be of no help whatsoever.

"Papa, we have to do something. We must go back and find his body or the hauntings are not going to stop. Somebody's going to get hurt before this ends. What happened to the boy? Who killed him?" Lila asked, closing her eyes as if she almost dreaded the answer.

Lila prayed it wasn't her Papa who was involved. That could get messy really fast. The boy might seek retaliation against her family.

"I don't know, but it wasn't me. I have never shot anyone. Must have been those rogues who lie in wait for the Indians to come down to trade. They must have gotten caught up in a skirmish."

"But I saw the spirit. The boy's too young to ride down with grown men. How did he get involved in a battle?"

"I don't know – I found the boy behind a thicket of bush, well out of sight behind an outcropping of big rocks that concealed his body. I had every intention to go back. I put him in a cave for protection until I could get back up there. I just never made it back."

149

"We have to do something right away. Otherwise, this is going to get out of hand. That boy has come back for vengeance. Someone killed him, and he's come back for revenge now. But the spirit seems to be protective of me. So maybe he won't hurt us. Maybe he is trying to protect me from something."

Levi went outside to see if his wife and daughter were okay, telling them it was safe to return to the house as the calamity was over. He couldn't bring himself to say the word ghost. But, slowly, he was buying into his younger daughter's theory. Lila hid the shoes under her bed, vowing not to wear them again. She knew a young warrior would do anything to protect his people. Those shoes were a symbol of his great people.

Lila lay in her bed. The darkness of the night enveloped her. There wasn't a sound to be heard except her sister's breathing in the bed next to her. She would have to do something quickly to protect her family. She wondered if there were any more restless spirits. Lila also wondered who had killed the boy? There were bad men in places. She had heard about the outlaws and how they lie in wait for Indians. The outlaw's conduct could ruin the peaceful relations the settlers had worked out following the war. This could disrupt everything they had worked so hard to establish. Finally, she drifted off to sleep with a plan to help her father.

Lila awoke with the ghost on her mind. How was she going to get her family to believe her? She feared it would take more destruction for them to buy into this ghost story. Her father wanted to explain away the mysterious circumstances by saying he didn't believe in ghosts of dead people.

That morning at breakfast, Agatha had already begun to rib Lila about Zack. The older sister still blamed Lila for taking him away from her even though Lila had never shown interest in Zack.

Lila's older sister continuously chided Lila, saying, "You better get caught up on your chores today. Any more time spent conjuring ghosts, and you're going to have a lot more messes to clean. I guess those dancing shoes aren't as great as you originally thought they were – and especially if they belong to a ghost!" Agatha howled in laughter.

"Agatha, please give it a break. I already told you I have no interest in Zack. To begin with, if you were more interesting, he might have more interest in you," she replied, feeling forced to take up for herself again. Lila let it go as she didn't want the spirit to intervene again on her behalf and possibly hurt her sister.

Flora chimed in, "Now girls, let's not argue at the table. We all know there's no such thing as ghosts and certainly not in this house."

Lila was beginning to feel helpless. Later that day, after finishing her chores outside, she returned to her bedroom. To her utter surprise, Lila found her sister dancing wildly in rhythmic patterns and foot stomping on their bedroom floor. To her amazement, she looked at Agatha's feet and saw the girl was wearing the dead boy's moccasins.

Horrified, Lila ran to her sister and begged her, "Give me those shoes. You don't know what you're doing!"

"I've got the shoes now," her sister shrieked. "You aren't the only one who can dance. And look at how good I am. Zack will fall in love with me again when he sees how beautiful I am."

At that moment, Zack appeared and was standing in the bedroom doorway with a basket of cookies.

"I brought you some cookies," he told Lila. Agatha glared at Lila while trying her best to dance closer to Zack to get his attention.

"What is your sister doing? She looks all crazy-like."

"She has taken my shoes and won't give them back," Lila confided. "Give me back my shoes, Agatha. You have no idea how much trouble you are inviting. This could be dangerous for us all."

"I'd say it's getting a little wild in here, wouldn't you, Zack? My little sister is going to find out the hard way that she's not the only girl with talent," screamed Agatha, laughing hysterically.

"Give them back to her, Agatha. They aren't your shoes, and you can't keep them," Zack yelled without smiling, showing support for Lila while believing the older sister had lost her mind.

Right then, Agatha fell to the ground as if something had tripped her. She cried out in pain as she lay on the floor of the room. Zack doubled over in pain as if he'd been punched in the stomach. Lila watched all this and was horrified over what might happen next.

Lila screamed to the invisible spirit, "Ghost boy spirit. Come to me, great spirit."

Then a big cloud of billowing mist appeared, followed by an image of the dead boy. Agatha and Zack each lay on the ground writhing in pain, but their eyes were filled with fright at what appeared before them.

"Speak to me. I command you to speak to me and tell me what my people have done to you, so we can make it right. We have caused you no pain. We mean you no harm. It's not my people who have betrayed and hurt you. Please, we bear no ill will toward you. Speak to me and tell me how we may help you," Lila pleaded with the ghost.

Things were escalating now to a point she realized something had to happen immediately. The mist formed a wraithlike shape which appeared before them.

A little boy's voice could now be heard, and in a dreadfully creepy voice, he said, "Little Happy Foot is my name, and your people took away my family. The settlers have destroyed Indians's values, land, and property. And now your father steals my shoes, and you dance like the great dancer I once was. And your people kill my people. You left me for dead, unburied, my spirit to wander forever. I have grown to love you but do not grow in like of your family. I protect you from those who hurt you and those who've done physical and unjust harmful things to me."

"But, wait, ghost boy. My people here have done you no harm, Little Happy Foot. I know we can make this right with you. I love your people and study much about you. I am like you — a lover of all things of nature and art. I call to you, oh great spirit, Little Happy Foot, to let us make right this wrong, that which has so cruelly been done to you," Lila pleaded.

With that, the cloud and voice disappeared. Agatha and Zack sat on the floor with their eyes open as big as saucers in disbelief of what they had just witnessed. But Agatha wasn't about to give in to her sister or a ghost.

"Oh, great spirit? Where in the world did you come up with such nonsense? You've been conjuring up horrid ghosts in our house. See, Zack, I told you she's like a little demon — like a witch," screamed Agatha, taking full advantage of the situation to show Lila to be a fool.

Ignoring her, Zack calmly responded, "I believe you, Lila. We must make a plan to return Little Happy Foot to his resting place. We need to get your father to help us. He might not ever believe Happy Foot is a ghost who now inhabits your home, but I believe it. We must do something right away."

Zack stayed until Lila's father returned from working in the field.

"Can you take us to the resting place of the mountain boy from whom you took the moccasins? Lila and I have an idea, but we need to go there really soon — maybe tonight?" asked Zack.

"I hope you two aren't still worried about ghosts," Levi laughed.

"Oh no, we're just curious about what happened to Little Happy Foot."

"Who's Little Happy Foot?" Lila's father asked.

"Oh, never mind," said Lila. "Just a name we made up to call the dead boy with the moccasins."

That night it was risky, but the three of them set out to walk a mile or so to the foot of the mountain plateau. Since the sun didn't set until late, there was plenty of time to make their way to the small cave. They walked inside, and Levi took them to where he had laid the boy. The boy's corpse still lay in the same place Lila's father had left him. A few weeks had passed, and the coolness of the cave had kept his body from total decay. Fortunately, Zack had carried along a shovel.

"We must dig a grave and bury his body before we leave. In honor of the dead. Or his spirit will wander forever as is their belief, so we must."

Levi, who once had every intention of coming back, agreed that it would not be right to leave the young boy unburied in the cave. The two males took turns digging the ground, now softened by rain, with the shovel until they had uncovered a hole large enough.

Gingerly, they placed his morbid body in the grave. Wanting to participate in the burial, Lila took handfuls of dirt and threw it

153

over his body while the males shoveled dirt over him until he could no longer be seen. Afterward, the three hurried home, now a bit spooked from the nightmare-like experience.

After returning home, Lila was sure everything would be okay now that Little Happy Foot was buried. But she would forever have a connection with the boy if only in her heart, for the little warrior had protected her. Now his spirit and gift of dance were forever awakened within her.

And from that day on, Levi forbid his family to ever speak of the dead boy or any belief in spirits.

*****

Years later, after Lila turned seventeen, she married Zack. Lila's older sister, Agatha, never forgave Lila for stealing Zack away from her, so the young couple was forced to move to another town settlement forty miles farther west. Lila bore Zack two daughters, whom they named Hattie and Lillian.

Agatha, who never married, died at the young age of twenty-five after contracting a virus in her late teens from which she never recovered. Lila's mother, Flora, took care of Agatha, who was bedridden, until her death. Levi and Flora remained in the town until they died.

Many years went by. The story lived on, passed down from one generation to another. The settlement grew over time, and to this day, in the dead heat of summer, mysterious happenings still occur at the site where Lila and her family once lived. And when they do, one can hear the constant barking of a dog in the distance.

And legend has it that the spirit of the Indian boy returns every year in search of the young girl with whom he once fell in love. And one generation after another explain to their children the story of the young boy who was killed and later buried. Children around campfires in every town shared the story of the boy and his restless spirit. And the ghost story, still told to this day, has become known throughout the region as the Legend of Little Happy Foot.

*****

Lillian was busy cleaning house and didn't want her daughter, Iris, who was playing dress up, to make a bigger mess than she already had.

"Dear, do get out of my closet and put those shoes away. Dress up time is over, and there's work to be done," the girl's mother said.

Iris sat on the floor of her mom's closet, and slowly removed the tape from around an old cardboard box, lifting off the top. Inside, the young girl found what appeared to be a pair of old worn suede shoes with laces strung in multi-colored beads. Cool, she thought. Delighted, Iris removed her own shoes and carefully pulled the soft suede snugly over her feet as the slippers were old and delicate. They were almost the perfect size for her. The girl stood up, excited to show her mother, when suddenly, she felt the most incredible urge to dance.

~~~~~

*The Legend of Little Happy Foot is in memory of my husband, Joseph Lloyd Sykes, whose drum beating, foot stomping, and finger tapping entertained folks for many years.*

~~~~~

As a writer, Stephanie Williams Dean has published numerous feature stories in newspapers, magazines, and newsletters. After many years working in the nursing profession, Stephanie retired and returned to school to earn a graduate degree in ministry. Stephanie enjoys writing from personal life experience to help inspire hope in those who suffer. She is currently editing her fiction novel, *Bred in the Bone*, while working on *Lykes, Lines and Loves*, a non-fiction, historical account of her dad's journey overseas as a Merchant Marine during World War II. Stephanie writes a food column, Bless Your Spoon, for the Davie County Enterprise Record.

## DEDICATION

All proceeds from the sale of this book will benefit the Hart Square Village in Vale, North Carolina.

## ACKNOWLEDGEMENTS

Special thanks go out to Karen Tillman for her instruction and support of Stephanie Dean Williams with some of the artwork in this book.

# Books by the Renegade Writer's Guild

Renegade Writer's Guild publishes anthologies with the middle-school-age reader in mind, donating the proceeds to benefit various services in North Carolina.

### *The Magic Horses of Crystal Creek Camp*
(Proceeds benefit the Davie County Public Library.)

### *Tales of Tails*
(Proceeds benefit the Davie County Humane Society.)

### *Haints, Haunts, and Hallowed Hills*
(Proceeds benefit Hart Square Village.)

Made in the USA
Lexington, KY
03 November 2019